Beautiful and Out Cold

This is a story of Beautiful in which her looks matched her name. She had a rich chocolate skin tone, dark green eyes and a body to die for. She was actually willing to have sex to secure a bag(money). She met her match when she started secretly dating her best friend's brother, Delano.

Delano had a past of selling drugs but washed it and was legit. He liked Beau's snooty attitude and she was young and sexy. He was going to make her his wifey whether she liked it or not.

This is an urban tale that is filled with drama. There will be a lot of sex and cursing.

Disclaimer:

This book is intended for mature audiences. This book might include cheating, rape, violence, drugs and physical and mental abuse.

I am The Most Controversial Romance Writer...I Dedicate All My Books To My Readers...

1. A Beautiful Virgin {intro}

 Beautiful: Stopppp I moaned as he kissed on my neck and then sucked on a sensitive spot. I was a virgin and dead set on staying one this night. Delano continued to massage my nipples through my thin cotton white tube top which I didn't have on a bra. It felt so good but I pushed him away as I leaned back tryna catch my breath. "Beau, why you teasing a nigga" he said frustrated gritting his teeth which the bottom four was platinum..he was fine as hell. He was 6'2 dark chocolate, a connected goatee and beard, deep set brown eyes, a low fade and a six pack..his build was thick and he was 27.

Okay before i go on i was BEAUTIFUL, Not bragging but i was thick asf @ 5'5, 38 dd,22 inch waist,40 inch hips all dipped in chocolate skin tone wit thick blk hair past my shoulders n green exotic natural eyes and a medium size nose in which i usually wore different nose rings. My name is Beautiful and I'm 19 years old. "I'm not teasing Delano, you wanted to talk to me i thought, not fuck" i said looking out the window of the passenger window. We were now sitting in his blk Camaro sitting on 26" blk rims.He had mad money, his family had gotten a huge 10 million dollar lawsuit when the police killed his brother four years ago. "Look, i want to be ya nigga! I can get you your own crib, give you money to shop but you be bullshitting man" he said pinching the bridge of his long sexy Tupac nose, he did that when he was annoyed. "Lano, first of all i told you we can't be more than friends, i'm not gonna mess up my friendship with Zaya " which was his sister. He had been secretly stalking me and crushing on me for the last year and he was becoming very aggressive!

2. Zaya Bday Party

After talking wit Delano in his whip, I got out after giving him a peck on the cheek." Damn shawty, ya ass phat" he said checking out my ass in my dark denim short stretchy shorts. I laughed and kept walking in my parents house. I had both my mother and father who married two years before I was conceived. My father was an Oral surgeon and my mother was a Nurse and they also had several businesses. I was an only child and very spoiled. I had graduated with honors from high school and was still tryna figure out what I wanted to be. We lived in Texas in a huge black gated community. We had a huge 6 bedroom home, 3 car garage and an outside swimming pool that I would invite friends over on weekends.

My parents trusted me prolly more than they should've. I drank Grey Goose, loved weed and I had a nice lil 2015 Jeep that was black. I got it for a graduation present. That weekend I had plans to visit and stay the weekend with Zaya at a hotel to bring in her 20 th bday party held at the 5 star new hotel 2 hours from our community. I had gone shopping so I could be the number one stunner! I decided to show up in a Nike black n white short set but ditched the Nike tee with a white wife beater knotted in da back to show o my newly healed tattoo that said "OUT COLD" on my lower back, all blk low top Forces, two thin gold necklaces, a few real gold bracelets n earrings and gold anklet. My hair was in a natural curly state but freaked out small braids in the front. "Bitch meet me outside " I said, pulling up to the hotel as soon as she said hello. "Ok, I'm on my way" she said excitedly. Zaya was light skin short blond haircut that stayed fresh, she was pretty with full pink lips and dimples just like Delano. After I settled in our huge suite we sat out our new clothes and bikinis.It was about to go down!

3. He Wants This Chocolate!

"Is Delano gonna be there" i asked as i hit a fire ass blunt Zaya had rolled up. "But of course, that is my brother"she said, taking down a shot of Henny." Bitch, don't get too fucked up, you don't want to miss your own party" i said. We had the whole 8th floor of the Four Seasons Hotel and we reserved a room on the main floor that had pool tables, big screens everywhere, big fluffy leather couches and an inside pool.

I had on a black 2 piece bikini set on but had on some white jeans shorts over the bottoms and some white on white low top Adidas. I just had my hair up in a high curly ponytail and some big hoop gold earrings. My cell went off. Damn this hoe ass nigga i said to myself putting it to voicemail. It was Quan crazy ass! This nigga had mad money but he was too much for me.

Last time i hung out with this nigga he was off them beans(extasy pills) and had put a gun to a dude head that tried to holla at me at a liquor store we had went to so he could get me some Goose and pineapple juice and some Ciggarellos . I had never went past getting my titties sucked on so i had to be very picky about what niggas i spend my time with. We went down to the Entertainment room and made sure the DJ had arrived.."Look, all I want you to play is Trap music and RnB" Zaya told DJ Black. You know his black ass was all over our young tender asses."Aye Beau, you need to holla at me" he said grinning. "You're too old to handle all this" I said, putting an extra twist to my hips and his tongue was wagging. Shiddd, the party was in full effect @ around 11:30 and i was kicking it with Rell cute ass.We went to highschool together and we dated for almost all of junior year.

We broke up after too many fights about me holding out the Pussy . "You still got da pussy on lock" he asked in his sexy thick deep voice that made old n young hoez moist. "Yeah I'm still waiting for Mr Right not right now, you feel me" Actually i don't, I'ma be a fucking doctor in less than 6 years and you don't wanna fuck with a educated nigga, you want a thug" he kinda yelled."Damn my baby, you still mad tho" i said walking off in another direction.

 I was tryna avoid Delano . Being the boss that I was, I gave my girl Zaya a gift card at a hair shop that did zillions, hair extension fusion, sew-ins etc..but anyway it was $500 on the gift card. I ran into a fake ass bitch that we had gone to school with named Leesa. She was one of dem hoes that will fuck a snake with no head! . Foreal foreal. "Heyyy Beau" she said, passing me a blunt."Umm I'm good, I didn't see that bitch get rolled" i said with my nose turnt up. Bitch you got me fucked up i was thinking. Before the hoe could respond Delano walked up."What it do lil mama" he asked looking down at me. Leesa was like "I'm good, trying to ride a black ass nigga dick tonight" . He chuckled and said "Damn baby girl, let a nigga live".

I had to laugh at how desperate and thirsty she was acting. Wowww."I can give you a preview in the back room" she said thinking he was turned on. "You cute lil mama but Beau more a nigga type, ya feel me" Damn! I thought as she just walked off, embarrassed."Delano, that was wrong how you did her and you know you're gonna get her number later" i said shaking my head.

 He grinned, showing them platinum bottoms."You think you know me, sexy" he asked. "Whateva nigga" i said looking at my freshly done today french manicure. "Why are you always looking so sexy" he moaned, spinning me around for his inspection."Boy stop" I laughed. I loved attention from him but i felt like he was fucking all these hoes, got bread,n he was fine and from what i heard he laid pipe .

4. Hating Ass Bitches

"At Least give a nigga a hug" he said grabbing me. I hugged him back and i felt his erection." Every time I see you, that happens" he breathed in my ear. I got wet as he leaned in and tongued the shell of my ear."Stop, you are so nasty" i said, wiping the light layer of saliva out of my ear . "Delano, i was wondering where the fuck you was at negro" One of his hoes Tish said.

She was a drunk ass bitch, pretty, but a drunk ass bitch! She was his age so you know she tried to debow me."And what the fuck you doing in my nigga face, young ass lil hoes i swear" she said taking a sip of her drank . "Bitch, don't come at me, holla at ya nigga, he up in my face" i yelled, getting crunk. "Tish, take yo ass to the car, you on dat drunk ass shit"he said disgusted.

Zaya had walked over and was ready to do whateva and that's why I fucked with her. "Get this hoe out my party" she said to Delano. As he dragged that hoe out we were laughing our asses off. We twerked all night long and eventually got in the pool and smoked blunts rolled by me and sipped on some 1738. I was more of a white liquor drinker but fuck it! The night ended well into the morning and i fell asleep on my temporary bed drunk as fuck but by myself. We made it home the next day on Sunday. I wasn't really into these churches but I definitely believed in God. I kicked it with my mom and dad, told them the nice part of my trip and went to my plush ass room decorated in a leopard print theme bedroom. You know I had silk and satin sheets, 60 inch plasma mounted on the wall and in the closet new clothes with tags still on them. A bitch barely wore the same thing twice.. I went into my connected bathroom decorated in zebra print down to my toothbrush.

I took a shower and before you know it i was rubbing my nipples thinking about Delano. Oooh, I had an itch that needed scratching. I ran the soapy rag between my sweet tender thick chocolate thighs. Damnnnnn, i needed some dick in my life.

5 . Where the Smoke At??

I knew I had to do something as far as income real soon because I had to get my own crib so I could lay up if I wanted to and come and go in peace . It had been two weeks since Zaya party and I was working in my parents medical supplies small store which was growing everyday with ppl coming in and ordering wheelchairs, orthopedic shoes, diabetes needles and so on. They paid me nice but I didn't like customer service and that was a must!

 I was naturally talented in keeping up with the money . In walked Zaya. "What's going down" she asked looking cute in a Puma short set that was red and white and she had the lil Pumas to match. "You look cute" I said. " Girl this shit old as hell" she laughed.

I can't stand when hoes do that, bitch just take a compliment ! "Bitch old or not, you look cute" I said annoyed. "Thank you lady" she said scrolling through her phone. "Umm, you know Leesa have a gig this weekend right" she asked. "I really don't fuck with her like that and you know that shit bitch" i spat out. "Come over and have a drink after work and a few blunts" she grinned. "I do need to hit a blunt" I said. "Ain't no one here, come to my whip real quick and get a puff, i got a half a blunt out there" she said. "Damnn" i said looking right at the camera. The struggle was real and weed made me think instead of being bored and watching the clock. I had on a jade green sundress that was strapless, tight at the breast part leaving out a nice view of cleavage and it flared out a few inches above knees and I had on a nude brown thin cardigan over it and nude brown four inch pumps.

I dressed accordingly to my job. After hitting the blunt my day went a lil smoother and i closed down the store for the day.We made almost ten racks today. I was gonna suggest getting a part time security guard to my parents.

Later that day i had my Jeep detailed and as i waited i went next door to a Soul food diner. You get a meat of your choice, 2 sides and a dessert and soda fa $10 out da door. I ordered fried wings,chicken dressing, baked mac and five cheeses and sweet potato pie. As I was eating in came Delano! "How you doing sexy" "Fine and you" I smiled looking at his sexy ass. He sat down next to me and ordered the same thing I had ordered.

6. The Deal Layed Out!

I had been avoiding him since the party. How he gonna be kissing all on me and he was with another bitch, yeah whatever! "Why you spinning a nigga shawty" He said sliding in the booth with me. Damnn, he smelled good and looked so good in the black fitted cap that had gold writing that said "KING" . A black tee not tight but you could see his nice form and some dark denim slightly baggy jean and black n gold J's. To top it off he had a gold chain with a nice size "jesus piece" swinging almost reaching his dick..Swagged out! "You look really sexy" I told him.

 I couldn't help but be drawn to raw masculinity. He was a dark ass nigga but i could tell he was blushing. I was young but very charming and wise for my years. I knew men loved compliments as much as women." You thought about what we talked about he asked. That's why I was up here. He had called and I really didn't have shit to do so I answered and he said come holla at him and I got a top of the line detail and dinner on him.

"Yeah, I've been thinking about it but you think you can deal with someone my age who wants to hang out and party" I asked. " I want that "he pointed towards under the table at my privates. "Besides you act older and more mature than females my age" he said. "So you ain't in no relationship" I asked cautiously. I fuck these hoes but it ain't serious" he said. "But if I give up my virginity to you, I want to be just me and you sexually, too many diseases out here." I said disgusted. "It's whateva you say baby" he said slyly. "Plus i want it on the down low until we both feel comfortable" i said. We made plans to have dinner and talk more about it on Friday.

 "This is a start "he said, handing me a knot of money . "Very good start" I said thinking about shopping at the new mall that had a grand opening a week or so ago. I gave him a long wet kiss as he felt on my hips and ass. After he walked out, I counted the cash, it was $785. Not bad and i hadn't fucked him yet..

7. She won't but then again,maybe she will

 Delano: I was so fucking tired of begging this bitch for that pussy! I was gonna get it and dog that bitch! She fucking with a real nigga. I was obsessed with her fine ass. I had moved back to Texas after living in Arizona for 5 years building my empire. I had gotten a loan from my dad to get my business off the ground and was doing pretty well.

With my dope money and the loan, I had become fully legit.

Even though I had a southern drawl and accent I had a business masters degree. Beautiful had been at one of the family bbq's and she was in a fitted Cap that was white, a red thigh high tight body dress and played down with some red and white Forces. I WANTED her as soon as I laid eyes on her.

 She was young but so ready. I had seen her but never paid attention to her because she was so much younger, 8 years to be exact. I hadn't realized i was staring until my then girlfriend Aaliyah waved her palm in my face."Shit girl, stop playing. I swatted her hand. "You wanna fuck that lil hoe " she yelled. "Man chill out" i said trying to calm her down. Her light skin face was turning red from anger. Now that i looked at her , she really wasn't all that pretty and niggas fucked with her because she had a ok body and she was mexican and black. I usually went for the lighter skin toned women but i was instantly attracted to Beau this time when i saw her.

 Her weave(didn't know it was her natural hair pressed out) was straightened under the fitted cap and I could see how she was ghetto, polite, funny, confident and sexy. I walked over and introduced myself. She was talking to her friend, my sister and a dude was goggling her goods in that dress. "Damn you so fine" dude was saying as i put in my two cents "Can you afford a woman like this" i asked him.

He knew a real KING and he walked away head down. I was iced the fuck out! Watch,ears and neck iced out and my bottom four platinum blinging "Beau right" i asked. "Delano right" she said sarcastically. "I just wanted to tell you, that you are the most beautiful woman I've seen besides my moms" I grinned showing my dimples that made hoes so wet. She acted unfazed by my swag. "Thank you" she said unbothered. The fuck!!! "Yeah so you are coming to the car show next week" I asked, taking in all that chocolate beauty and thick full lips . She said "Depending who asks me to go" she said. "Come fuck with a real nigga, what you drank" i asked and that's how we started talking.

8. Quanny crazy ass!

I was at the mall shopping for a new fit when I chill with
Delano this Friday and I ran into Quan crazy ass! I was
nice to him because he was a ticking time bomb . "Hey
Quan" I said, a bit nervous. "Damn baby, why you spinning
a nigga" he grinned looking high as fuck the way his eye
was low. "Shidd, I just been handling my business and

working and shit" i said. A guy passed and was staring at me and i was lovely so i didn't see the problem and Quan was like "Disrespectful ass nigga" showing his gun tucked in his pants to the dude.

"Hey chill Quan, we in the mall" I said, calming him.. We only kicked it a few times and he was acting as if we was dating, the fuck! He ended up buying me a few fits and some J's as a sorry the way he acted last time gifts . He was cool as long as he wasn't gone off the beans (X pills) .

I ended up going over to Zaya's crib to smoke a couple blunts of the weed that Quan had given me. I brought over some juicing items so Zaya could put her juicer to work. I loved juicing, it helped tame my weight, flushed out toxins and I got my nutrients faster than eating the fruits and veggies. I juiced us some carrots, celery, ginger and some cucumbers . She hated the taste and I figured if I could drink a shot of Liquor, why not drink something healthy. "So I just saw Quanny crazy ass! He was on chill mode today tho" i   laughed. "I think someone slipped him a mickey cause he be acting weird as fuck" Zaya said rolling the blunt.

 I walked Delano and his homeboy that I was crushing on for the longest, Carlos. I was glad I had on an off one shoulder half tee with slashes through it showing off my yellow bra underneath and some white ripped jeans and some yellow 3 inch strappy sandals and you know my toes were on point with a nice design consisting of white and black and gold.

"What it do sexy" Delano said smiling."Shit chillin, smoking " i said hitting the blunt. "How yall young ladies doing" Carlos asked. I had to play it off and shit because Delano was watching my response and he knew that Carlos was a ladies man also.

He was Puerto rican with that honey brown complexion and with long wavy hair that stayed freshly braided and he had money , a 3 year old son and he was 26 . "What's good with you" Zaya said, answering for us.. I just nodded politely and shyly. Carlos made my pussy so wet.

9. Beautiful Deflowered

Beautiful: It was Friday and I met Delano at his crib which was a huge four bedroom ranch style home with the traditional white with black siding and I liked the black shutters on the windows. His lawn was fenced in and the landscaping was on point with flowers and all. For our first real date we were going to the newly built casino . It was 2 hours away but I was so excited and hoped I won some loot.

 I had on some designer jeans that was tight as fuck, a custom made half shirt that was orange and said #1 STUNNA in gold letters, and my Baby Phat Orange high top shoes and my designer leather purse which was orange. And you know that orange looked good on my chocolate skin. "Damn girl, you're so fine" he said spinning me around to check me out. "I love this" he said running fingertips on my tat on my lower back.

 "Thank you" I said, giving him a hug and you know the dick was wooded up. "I hope you can handle this dick baby, i'll be gentle" he whispered in my ear. I hoped I could handle it also. He had sent me many dick pics over the last few days that i definitely enjoyed and he was thick and long. I had agreed to let him be my first because he was getting me my own crib and I needed that. Don't get it twisted, i had around 12 racks saved, but he was offering a crib, shopping sprees and good sex, shit, why not?? I was ready for some steamy hot sex with this experienced sexy man. It was human nature to want to be filled up as a woman. As he drove we talked about different things and I told him my family thought I was spending the weekend over Zaya's crib.

"And no, Zaya has no idea it's you I'm hanging out with" I said before he asked. I had already explained i wanted to be low-key until i was comfortable with our lil arrangements. I could've worked my ass off and got my own crib but i didn't want those responsibilities and I was gonna continue to stack my bread . He also told me that his 3 recording studios were making a nice bit of money. "I know I got you by 7 or 8 years shawty, but I just wanna spoil you and treat you like the Queen you are" he told me. "Thank you Delano" I said shyly.

He was laying it on real thick. "All i do is think about laying between them thick chocolate thighs" he said as we pulled up to the casino and got valet parking which he gave the valet dude a $5 tip. "Let's go win" he said grinning showing his dimples. He wanted to play together and shit so i sat on his lap at a $1 slot machine and the max was $5 and you know i play max. His dick was on hard majority of the time and i loved the way it was rubbing between my ass as i squirmed on his lap. I was gonna let him fuck me tonight.

Part 9 And A Half

I hit the 7's which was $1500 and he had put in about $500 in different slots. I tried to give him half and he told me it was shopping money for me. Coo!! We decided to stay at the beautiful casino hotel because after we ate dinner at one of the casinos restaurants it was going to be 2am. He had been kissing on me, holding my hand, and caressing my ass all night and I was wet and ready. He had bought me a couple of drinks so I was a lil bit looser than usual and I knew he had some smoke . We got to our deluxe suite and it was gorgeous with huge windows that looked over the city, a small but nice kitchenette, a huge bed with silk bedding that was red and mirrors above the bed.

But my favorite was the huge hot tub in the massive bathroom totally separate from the shower that had a mirrored sliding door. I felt him come behind me and I was nervous." Let me love you" he moaned in my ear. He was kissing my neck and then sucking on the spot, he kissed then lightly nipped. "Oooh" i moaned. He laid me on the sink counter which the light was on a dimmed lighting, making it very sensual to be kissing this sexy fine ass nigga! " Let's take a shower" I suggested. I wanted to be completely clean and virginal when he took this pussy. I undressed in front of him showing all my curves and imperfections but he said "You are perfect" as he fucked me with his eyes. He also undressed in front of me and I loved his toned muscular thick body but his dick was the best. It long , veiny and thick chocolate. It seemed to have a mind of its own as it pointed towards me as he walked towards me. We got in the hot water stream of the shower and we bathed each other and we both brushed our teeth and used the mouthwash the hotel had as a complimentary give as the chocolate covered strawberries next to the bed.

I stroked his dick and he guided me and taught me how to please him as he rubbed my hard dark berry nipples. "Damn bby, you a natural "he said as he sucked on my breasts while caressing my so but firm ass cheeks sneaking in a finger to massage my trimmed but unshaved pussy lips. " Oooh" I moaned as he gently rubbed my opening. We got out and he helped me towel dry my hair and carried me to the bed. I didn't know what to do. I was excited and scared.

Part 9 Continued

He laid on top of me between my thighs."Beautiful i got you now" he whispered and i loved his hard thick body on me. The lights was on but dimmed and i looked up and seen the erotic picture we made with him on me and my hand lightly digging into his back. He was kissing a slow wet journey down my tummy and he licked in around my belly button. "Pleassse" i begged for his tongue not to stop. He kissed my thighs that was open and trembling. I held my breath.

 All I felt was his long velvet tongue lapping from my clit to my asshole as he lifted my thighs to his shoulders."Fuckkkk, it feels so goodddd"i cried out. He gave my pussy the best french kiss a girl could get lightly nipping on my lightly hair covered lips and then attacking my sensitive nub and i took that pleasure for less than three minutes and all i felt was my body tensing and releasing and i actually seen stars as i felt my body jerking and twisting and i knew i was having my first Orgasm.

 I looked up and he said something but i was dazed as i felt something hard poking at my sensitized opening. He thrusted in my wet tightness to the hilt and I screamed from pleasure but mostly pain." Ahhh, you are so wet and tight" he moaned in my mouth. "It hurts" I cried out not noticing the tears coming from my eyes until he kissed them away. "I'm sorry" he said moving gently in and out. He kissed me gently as he moved his hips in different angles as he told me how tight and good I felt and I was just ready to get this full feeling gone.

He was packing and it was uncomfortable. He soon was pumping harder in and out and faster and he bust all in that tight gripped pussy moaning my name " Beau Beau Beau" as he closed his eyes tightly and gripped the sheets on both sides of my head. Wow i thought as i instantly fell asleep and he fell to the side of me and we spooned and cuddled. Damn he fucked me so good..

10. Delano

Delano: "Ahhh, you so fucking wet baby" i said to Beau as i slid my throbbing dick into that tight wet cavity. This was the tightest pussy I had ever had and she was definitely a virgin. "It hurts" she cried. I didn't give a fuck, i was busting tonite and fulfilling my fantasy of over a year. I looked down and saw her tears and kinda felt bad "I'm sorry" I said moving slowly and steady but her pussy was clenched around my achy dick. "Fuck me back" i whined in her ear as i put my hands under her and gripped that phat ass as i long dicked her.

She was whimpering and i felt that pre orgasm feeling building "Ahhh, Beau Beau Beau" i moaned out as my Orgasm came in waves as all my strength came out my dick and coated her creamy insides as i jerked and buried my head in her neck.

I stayed in her for a few minutes to collect myself. Shawty done pussywhipped a nigga already i thought as i pulled out my dick from her cum soaked pussy and pulled her into my arms and fell into a blissful blackness. I know she was sore but my dick hurt from her tightness and I wanted to be in those tight pink chocolate folds again. She was still asleep and looked so beautiful as her given name. I was getting soft on her and that wasn't good. I mentally thought about how I never gave bitches shit but dick and an occasional $100 bill. I knew i was a fine ass intelligent brotha with money and i could have just about whoever i wanted but Beautiful was different. Innocent, mean to me,sexy, always seemed annoyed with me, good pu$sy.

 I guess it was her confidence and she was a challenge! I had to take it slow and make her fall for me as I had already fallen for her, I thought as she said "I gotta pee"and wincing from her newly penetrated pussy that was sore as she got out of bed. "Omg!, Delano all this blood" she panicked as she walked in the bathroom and sat on the toilet.

 It was blood and cum all on the silk sheets.I walked in the bathroom naked as she was on the toilet. "Get out" she said embarrassed. I left out chuckling but not before I saw dried blood and cum on her thighs. It turned me on that I had cum in her and she could possibly be pregnant. Okay, yeah i was falling hard for her. I heard the shower running and I came back to the bathroom and I slid in the shower with her."Will you be my girlfriend"

11. He did that

Beautiful: "Will you be my girlfriend" I felt him come in the shower behind me and thank goodness I had cleaned myself before he got in. "You okay shawty" he said rubbing my shoulder as hot streams of water covered us both. I turned in his arms and soaped a new rag and bathed his dick and it grew harder and longer as I stared at it stroking it, loving the way it felt. "Ahhh, I want that pussy tho" he said, lifting me up and sucking my already hard nipples. "Yesss" I moaned. I was sore but yearned for some more Orgasms. I wrapped my legs around his waist and he slid his dick in my tightness. "Fuck, you feel so good" he moaned sucking my earlobe and that made me vibrate on that thick dick.

 He was going in slow and teasing me. "How it feels" " Sooo good" I cried out as he hit that g-spot! "Ohhh, please please" i begged as he had me by my ass lifting me up and down while looking at my fuck faces. "Cum for me baby" he said loving the control he had making me beg. His dick swelled up and i came apart crying out " yes yes fuck me good" i begged. He started moving faster and harder and then he froze and I felt him throbbing over and over as his dick squirted in me at least ten times filling my pussy with its thick cream. After a few minutes he pulled out and my rubbery legs came from around his waist and we bathed all over again without talking. I slipped on my clothes after we had room service breakfast. I felt different. "You ok baby" he asked."Yes, just thinking to myself" i said patting my natural hair that was pulled into a ponytail to the back. I felt kinda shy after doing all those nasty things with him. "Don't feel shy around me" he said. "You got some A1 pussy" he chuckled.

12. Jealous Ass Nigga!

It had been a week since our casino trip and I was loving life but Delano was tripping about me wanting to be low-key. I wasn't trying fuck up my friendship with Zaya. She already told me he had fucked almost all her friends. But she figured he would leave me alone because he went for the light skin/ mixed females.

 I always wondered how she was light skin and he was dark. When I saw their parents it was no wonder. The dad was light skin and the mom was dark hershey colored. But they had a lot of the same features, long hawkish nose, deep set eyes and dimples. Anyways, he had been blowing my cell up! Damn, let a bitch live i thought to myself. I had seen him three times this week and I was going out this weekend with my girls.

 He wanted to Netflix and Chill. . Negro please! I had a bad ass dress I had bought with some of that casino money and the stilettos were out cold. I answered my cell "What it do?" i answered all sexy. "Zaya said yall was going to Pete's party this weekend" he said kinda with an attitude. "I was thinking about it" I said carefully, gauging his reaction. "I wanted to spend some time with you tho". He wanted to fuck! "And that's what's up but you know I'm young and not to be tied down". "Oh, it's like that" he asked, feeling clearly hurt. He wasn't used to rejection but he had never fucked with a bitch like me.Ya heard?? My mom hipped me to these niggas games and that's prolley why her and my dad was still passionately in love with her still to this day.

 What he didn't know is this bitch that Zaya introduced me to when we got our Pedicures, spilled some muthafuckin tea! "Gurllll, your brother ain't shit" Kia said laughing. Zaya had brought Kia along with her. Kia was a pretty honey brown skin tone female and she talked too damn much but seemed cool. "Bitch what? He fucking one of your friends" Zaya laughed. "Girl, he called me a few days back late as fuck, saying he wanted to talk and you know i told him to come over, we talked and FUCKED!" she laughed. "Ughh, I don't want to hear about my bra" Zaya said disgustedly. "Bitch, he ain't called me back, he plays too much" she said sadly .

I just sat back listening while the chinese lady massaged my calf with some kind of moisturizing lotion. That's why i was gonna do me, niggas wasn't shit. I was a good girl and look, he took my virginity and he gave me money but he was fucking other hoes. Fuck it! It was a business transaction. I'ma use these niggas until i feel like settling down and this was gonna be fun! I didn't realize how dumb and stupid i was thinking but oh would i regret a lot of shit.

13. Start of an Obsessive boyfriend!

Kia had did me a fucking favor! I was kinda hurt that the same night i turn him down for some pussy, he fuck the next bitch! Okay, I'm good tho. From that Thursday night until Saturday morning I hadn't talked to him. He had come by my job but we had a new dude that was a part time worker and he covered for me as I ran to the back when I saw Delano Camaro pull up in front of the store."Where is Beau" he asked in a bully sort of way.

"Umm, she went home for the day" Dexter said, stuttering and shit. "Man, tell her to fucking call me" he said walking out. I came from the back when Dexter called for me. " He crazy as fuck but he fine and so aggressive, my type" he said laughing. Dexter said he was Bi but i knew he loved a man! "Thank u Dex" I said , kissing his cheek.

This muthafucka texted me some shit as me and Dexter was closing down the store for the night. "I got the keys to your new place baby" Delano texted me. Damn, now what do i do? I thought. Okay, I'll act like shit sweet and do me behind his back. I wanted to still go to the party so I didn't respond. When I did talk to him, I would tell him what Kia had shared with us. I was a genius or I thought I was . Bitch, I'm ready" I said yelling from Zaya' s extra bedroom. I had told my parents that I was chilling over at Zaya's as they were going on a casino weekend trip anyways. I had hinted to them that I was thinking about getting my own place and they told me no matter what I would always be able to come home. Cool. "Damn bitch, you stuntin 'on these hoes" she said, taking in my leather white mini strapless dress and my white tie up around the calf leather 4 inch stilettos gladiator sandals.

"Thank you" I said, turning every angle in the full length mirror. "Bitch, don't get that pussy taken" she joked. We made it to the upscale club and I was under aged but Zaya's cousin worked security and we were let in free. Hoes was hating and niggas was jocking! I was gonna enjoy my night out.

14. No means No!

I was chilling sipping on my Grey Goose and pineapple juice, we had just come from smoking a blunt in the parking lot and I had spotted Carlos as I was coming from getting my lip gloss out of my whip, Delano homeboy i had the crush on. I acted as if I hadn't seen him and he walked up on me and was like "Hey, lil mama."Oh, hey Los" i said nervous. "Who are you with" I asked. "Don't worry, Lano ain't here with me" he chuckled.

"He ain't my nigga, so he do him, I do me" I said. "You look real sexy" he said as his gold colored eyes set me on fire as he looked at me from top to bottom. "You as well" I said slyly. " Who are you here with?" he asked. "Umm, just me and Zaya "Why are you out here by yourself". "It doesn't even matter but I'm about to go back in" I said , making sure my ass had an extra bounce and I knew he was looking.

I was asked to dance quite a few times but I was good. I got up at our table and danced a lil bit but I kept it classy and not trashy. After i was buzzed up i danced with a few niggas and you know they was tryna holla. "Bitch, I'm going to the ladies room" I told Zaya and she nodded. I was buzzed up real nice as I walked in the neatly clean restroom. Surprisingly it was empty. I handled my business and checked myself out in the mirror after washing my hands. Damn I was fine! I was ready to walk out and I was pushed back in there forcefully.

"What the fuck" i exclaimed. It was Delano! " Why did you dress all slutty? You trying fuck one of these hoe ass niggas" he gritted out using his body as a shield so i couldn't get out. I was in total shock. He locked the door and then he was trying to kiss me and shit. "No!, you acting fuckin psycho! Let me out" i said, struggling against him and he was getting hard and clearly turned on."No, I want some pussy" he said sliding up my mini."No, please stop, your drunk Delano" i begged. I smelled the Henny on his breath. Slap! "Shut the fuck up or else" he threatened.

I couldn't believe he slapped me and was forcing himself on me.

His handsome face was one of jealous crazy rage. He turned me around and bent me over the counter that had varieties of hand soaps. He yanked the strapless top of the mini dress down and pulled up the bottom over my thongs that was a lacy hot pink."Delano, please, let's leave here and do this" I whined. He ignored me as I heard him put spit on his dick and rammed it in me! I screamed out in pain but no one could hear if they wasn't in the bathroom. "You my bitch" he gritted out as he thrusted in and out. It had been a week since he had taken my virginity so i was still new to this and it hurt because i wasn't ready for this assault. He was giving all he had in a grudge fucking way, he was mad. "This my pussy! Ill kill you if you ever let another nigga in you" he said holding my small waist and fucking me hard and it hurt and was embarrassing.

He was gripping my breast as they was jiggling as he raped me raw and uncut! Some finally knocked on the door. "Come on, I gotta pee" a lady cried out. He ignored that and his thrust got faster and deeper. "Oh yeahhh" he moaned now gripping my tiny waist and pumping into me. "Ahh, Fuck! Damn this pussy good" he said busting and filling my pussy with his thick warm cream. "Now go home" he warned as he wiped his dick off with paper towel and walked out the bathroom with me bent over ass in the air and cum dripping slowly out of me.

 After he walked out I cleaned up as fast as I could and texted Zaya and said I was ready to leave! "Girl, I'm chilling , my guy friend will take me home, you okay" she said when I got back to the table.. "Yeah yeah I'm good" i lied. "Delano bought a couple bottles but his ass done disappeared" she said looking around in the club hoping to spot him." "Okay, I'm gone" I said, giving her a hug and walking out feeling weird and just totally shocked! I felt so many emotions that I can describe but dirty and embarrassed was a few.

15. A Chapter Of Delano

Delano: "What up my dude" Chance said, giving Delano some dap as he walked into the huge recording studio. "Shit my nigga, got you a tight ass beat "Delano chuckled. "What's been good" Chance asked. "Mane, to be honest this lil bitch I'm fucking got me tight" he said pinching the bridge of his nose. "Nigga, it's always a bitch with you" Chance said laughing. "Naw, the situation is serious!" "Ahh man, what is it mane" Chance asked. "This young bitch I'm fucking got me going nuts, shawty was a virgin but she got game" he said as if he was sick.

"Damn boss, shawty got you bent" Chance said "It happens to the best of us mane, remember when Lisa had me gone" he said. "Yeah but Lisa was a nasty hoe, Beau was a virgin but my nigga, i seen her at da club and she was looking so fucking sexy that i stayed in the background and when she went to the ladies room, i followed her, locked the door and kinda forced myself on her" Delano said looking sick.

"Whoa! Mane what she doing to get you so stressed, mane" Chance asked curiously. "She using me for money and to get a place in exchange for sex and she really don't like me" he said embarrassed. "Naw that can't be right, you get all the hoes and you got bands, and iced out" Chance said in disbelief. "Mane, I can't figure her out, I have been after her for a year and finally got it and now I'm fucked up"

"Nigga, you whipped or in love bro" Chance said disappointed his idol was slipping on his pimping. "Naw, i just gotta fuck her out of my system" he said more to himself than Chance. "Ay, let's get to work, mane, we make hits round here" Delano laughed. He tried not to think about him raping her, he had never forced a female, they threw themselves at him. I knew how to get back on her good side tho. Money and the keys to the crib I got her. I could fuck her sexy ass and control who she fuck wit. Yeahhh i got this all under control i thought to myself.

16. Bitch Gonna Have To Be Fake As Fuck!

I was disgusted and angry about Delano! I mean, damn, you gonna rape me in da club!. He was so fuckin evil and controlling. I was just gonna use his ass from now on.

Foreal foreal.. I finally picked up his call on Wednesday. "What it do" I said, all slick and sexy at the same time. "Shawty, I'm sorry, I let my dick rule me" he said sounding sincere. "Was you stalking me or something? I didn't know you were there" i asked curiously.

"I watched you dancing with that hoe ass nigga, dressed all slutty" he said mad! "Delano, do you have the keys to my place" I asked. "That's why I was blowing you up shawty, I got the lease and keys for a year for you". "Foreal, Lano" I asked all excited to be grown in my own shit. "Yeah, but remember, you only fuck me and no niggas that ain't kin to you in that apartment" he explained. "Ok, I need to do some shopping for furniture and I got a king size bed and bedroom suite on fleek" I said. "I got you, my homeboy owns a nice furniture store" he said.

I screamed on the phone, whoo hooo! We talked about when he would take me shopping for my place. I put the rape to the back of my mind. That weekend I went furniture shopping and to the movies and dinner. He had given me a diamond and gold bracelet out of the blue. He had come unannounced at my job and took me to lunch and nervously gave me the bracelet. "Aww, thank you bby" I said as he put it around my milk chocolate delicate wrist.

"Can I bust you tonight? " he whispered at the movie theater. He was rubbing my left hand as I sat on his right in the cushiony laid back premium seat.. "I don't want a baby" I whined. "Only once won't hurt anything," he said trying to convince me. "I did hold my end of the bargain". "Are you serious?, and it only take one time to get pregnant" i said not believing what this negro was asking.

This was going left. "I got all my stuff pretty much packed, so what, you gonna be coming by just to get some pussy" i asked. "Naw, i work a lot but I'ma want to spend time with you and do thangs other than fucking you" he hissed out. "I'm just asking Dee" "Okay you giving a nigga a new name now huh" he asked laughing. "You so extra" I breathed out. He dropped me off and I went into a deep relaxing dreamless sleep ..

17. Bitch I Need A Place To Stay!

Me and Delano had gone to my new townhome which was a two bedroom with a newly remodeled basement with a wet bar. My bedroom was huge with a balcony for late night rendezvous with my boo! The furniture was being delivered and he had paid for my bedroom suite, artwork my mom had surprised me with to decorate my walls and tons of luggage and bathroom and kitchen accessories to be moved.

I was so good. My parents thought I had saved and had gotten the place by myself. Not!. My parents had deposited $5,000 in my savings and gave me a monthly $1500 on a Mastercard. I knew I could always come back home. Lil did Delano know, he had created a beautiful monster .

 I was gonna do whatever I wanted when he was out of town on business. Later on that day while getting new toiletries at Target, I got a text from Zaya. "Bitch, i need a place to stay" Damn, I ain't moved in yet and motherfuckers are already asking to move in! And not to mention i'm trying to keep me and Delano a secret! I called this bitch to see what the fuck going down ova there..

"Girl, what's up with your place" I asked. "I wanted that Gucci bag and my dude said he was gonna come through and you know how that went and I got an eviction notice" she whined. "Can I let you borrow the money and you pay me back" I suggested. "Shit better yet, Delano got money, get it from him" I also suggested.

"He always talks shit about me and my bills and plus you need a roommate to help your mall shopping ass" she giggled. "Bitch, whateva, I'm good and plus i got a new boo and we need alone time". "Bitch what?, Get that dick!" She laughed. "How much do you need to get caught up " I asked. "I need $2400 to get completely caught up"she moaned. "Ok, I'll be over there after i leave Target". " Thank you bestie" she sang out as I hung up.

I got to checkout and I ran straight into Quanny. "Hey boo" I said, giving him a hug. "My Bae" he said, squeezing me. "Me and 50 other girls" I said feening to be jealous. He ate that shit up laughing. "Damn Beau, you doing some serious shopping" he said as the cashier bagged his tire cleaner he bought. "Yeah for my new place" I said grinning. "He pulled out his black card and told the cashier to ring up my tab on his card. " Thank you" I said as he swiped the card for the $243.58 bill. He walked me outside to my car as we passed his old school sitting on some 30" chrome rims.

"Damn that bitch sexy" i said. "You can drive it whenever you want to, baby" he said grinning. After he put the items in my trunk, i gave him a tight hug and thanked him again and we made plans to hook up this weekend. He slapped my round ass and took off jogging before I could scold him. Damn Quanny was looking real sexy as he dipped off in his old school whip..

18. Young And Free!

I had been at my crib for a week and a half and had no company besides Delano fucking me day and night. I loved it but a bitch needed a housewarming party. I called

Zaya to plan it. I had met a few of my neighbors and Neesy was cool as hell and her man Ke'van was nice. They was in their mid 20's and both had really good jobs at Chrysler where they met. She was tryna hook me up with her brother Roe. Roe had dough but that was too close to home. Delano was too jealous and crazy to be dealing wit niggas close to home. "Bitch wassup" Zaya said, answering her cell. "Girl, I need you to help me with my lil gig on Saturday". "Okay, I'll come over in about, give me an hour, Keno ova here" i could hear her grinning.

 She loved that nigga, he was cute with bread but he had mad hoes."Okay bitch, call when you on ya way. Delano stepped through the door and this nigga had stayed every night with me and i was happy because i wasn't used to this bitch yet and when it got dark i was really scared.

 "Hey bae" I said, hugging him."Damn I'm hungry as hell, ain't ate shit all muthafuckin day!" he said, frowning. "Take me to go get some steak, asparagus, and potatoes" I said. "We can get a veggie burger to share to hold us over" he suggested. "Hell yeah, let's share a veggie patty from Subway" i said. Knock knock knock! "I bet that's Zaya" I said hitting the blunt he had sparked up.

I opened the door and it was Zaya. "Who in the new Coupe out there" she asked, wiggling her eyebrows. "Bitch, your brother, he brought me some weed" i said loud enough for him to cosign."Bro, you know i be blowing em, why you ain't say you the weed mans." Zaya asked with a attitude."That's why you can't pay your bills, shopping, fucking with lame ass broke niggas and all that shopping and weed!" he laughed.

"Whateva, girl, this party's gonna be the shit" Zaya said excitedly. "What party" Delano asked. "I'm having a housewarming party and you can help bra" I said slyly, looking at him. "Bitch, you gonna invite that fine ass nigga Tone" she asked. "Bitch, you already know" i said forgetting he was my sponsor. "Invite some thick redbones" he said . "Fa' sho, my baby" I said laughing.

He was salty but i was gonna have fun playing with him. I worked long 12 hr shifts at my parents store but at least I was my own boss and Dexter was there the last 6 hours everyday we were open which was Monday- Friday. Anyways, I invited Dexter but he was going out of town with his married boyfriend. So Friday hit and I went and got a few party favors like a couple gallons of Grey Goose, a gallon of Henny and a half keg of Budweiser. Delano had given me a zip of gas weed and shopping money so you know a bitch was gonna be da freshest.

 I loved my crib, it was so homey already and my parents had come to visit and they loved it! That Friday night Delano came through with Carlos. "Aye i got some gas, call your home girls for my nigga so he ain't looking at you" he said low in my ear. I had on a black leather jumper that was shorts and some gladiator sandals that came to my knees that was black leather also and I had on a gold hair chain and I had straightened my hair and let it fall over my shoulders.

 I was a fine ass woman. "Ima call Tomica". Tomica was a hustling ass bitch that stripped on and off depending on her money situation. The bitch was honey mustard complexion, white blond weave past her ass and natural light grey eyes with a bad ass body, but that hoe couldn't keep a man. She was a bad bitch but had a bad reputation but i fucked with her, she was cool as hell and we both loved to shop.

19. Bish, He Wants You!

 Shit we got crunk in that bitch. Tomica had come over looking pretty as hell in a red bodysuit and black stilettos. "Tomica this is Carlos and you know Delano " I said knowing Delano had been to "Diamond Katz" more than a few times and seen her strip. "Hi fellas" she flirted. Carlos and her conversated while Delano was tryna fuck. "Aye let them do they thang, you got me hard as fuck" he said spinning me around loving my thick body. "Boy stop" I laughed.

I noticed Carlos kept looking over at me with lust but maybe I was wishing or this gas had me tripping. Hmm, let me see what it is I thought to myself. "Play some music bestie" Tomica said. We weren't besties but i'll play this game.

I let her do her and you know how hoes get stupid when dicks around. I had Future mixtape playing on YouTube through my PS4 on the 65" plasma screen mounted to the wall. We had some shots of Goose and that hoe got really loose. Almost busted her head tryna pussy pop on a head stand drunk. We were laughing our asses off. Now usually that was her signature stripper move but the hoe was too drunk". "Carlos, I want you to cum in my mouth cause you are too muthafuckin fine" Tomica said an hour later. "Bitch, you tripping, matter fact i need y'all to go so i can fuck my man" i said bluntly, this hoe or any hoe will never run my house" Hell yeah, get this drunk hoe out my young lady house" Delano said disgusted. After they left, Delano drove us to Ihop and we had breakfast and just talked and laughed about the night's events.

I had rescheduled my housewarming party because Zaya wanted to have a toy party at her crib and plus i was tired anyways so it wasn't a big deal. The next day i heard my phone ringing and it was Tomica. "What it do" i answered. "Gurl, that nigga Carlos Fine as hell but he want your ass bad as hell, bitch i told the nigga i would suck his dick and he was like "Naw, but see if you can get my digits to Beau" she said mad.

"Girl damn, i cant talk right now but I'ma call you back asap" I hung up and hoped Delano didn't hear that shit. "Baby, who was that" He asked, laying on top of me naked with just his silk boxers on. "Tomica asked if she left her stunners" i lied. "Stop hanging with hoes like that foreal Beau, she out there bad" he said. "Yeah, you prolly done fucked her" i mumbled getting up to pee. "That ass fat" he said slapping one of my plump chocolate ass cheek. "Stoppp that hurt Lano! " i said pulling on my thigh high pink silk robe. I didn't know how to feel about Carlos being sneaky. I had always liked him but i never let on that i did. All these niggas wanted this chocolate and i couldn't blame them... I was Fine as hell and yes i knew it. As Delano fucked me i thought about Carlos on top of me and i came real hard on Delano dick as he moaned out my name.

20. DON'T GET CAUGHT

I wanted to be on a dolo solo move tonight but i needed a alibi so Delano wouldn't suspect nothing. That dude was on a bitch head. It was Thursday and i was going out with Zaya. She was picking me up and you know i was stunning. I had on a red bodysuit made with that stretchy material that clung to your body. I slipped on some white 4 inch pumps and grabbed my white leather designer bag. My hair was pressed reaching the middle of my back. Bish what? My skin was glowing under that sexy blood red body pantsuit. The bodysuit had a heart neckline so my titties was sitting up nice and full.

It was one of Delano homeboys parties. " Bitch, spark the blunt" Zaya said pulling into a not too far away space. " Girl this muthafucka seem lit" i said taking a pu. " Delano was asking was you coming" Zaya said. He had told me he wasn't going when i had asked him, i thought to myself. We left a half a blunt for on the ride home in the ashtray. We walked up and got in because Zaya cousin was the bouncer. The club was three story building and expensive decor. We decided to go up to VIP because Zaya said a dude she was fucking was up there and had told her to come up. We was welcomed by all dem horny ass niggas. I was all in. A fine ass nigga that was iced out with caramel skin tone was hollering at me hard as fuck and i was playing the game with him. " Damn shawty, when can a nigga take you out" he said. His name was shawn. " I love your bluntness" i giggled. He had Goose on ice and Belvedere. We was kicking it until I seen Delano out the corner of my eye. Hmmm, this was gonna be a interesting night i thought downing my drink. " This my shit" i said out loud. " Lets dance" Shawn said grinning.

We went to the dance floor passing Lano and some latino girl he was hugged up on. Zaya was kicking it with some cute ass dark nigga. Delano hadn't seen me yet. Niggas ain't shit, i had told him i wasn't coming and he had told me the same. Oh well. I freaked him and he was coming right back at me, grinding his dick against my ass and shit. " I wanna fuck you mami" he whispered in my ear. I grinned and grinded on him. After 2 songs we walked back to our table and i felt hot blazing eyes on me. I was glad it was really dim in the club." Bitch, i just rolled, let's smoke" she laughed. " Girl, im having fun" i laughed also. We lit up right in VIP. I was keeping a eye out for Delano. He was a lil touched(crazy asf). Shawn slid in the booth with us. I looked up as i seen Delano walking towards our table with that latin looking gurl. " Me and Shawn was talking shit and laughing. " What it do?" Lano said darkly. " Ah man, what it do Lano?" Shawn said not knowing me and Lano was fucking.lol. " Shit Nigga, getting money and pussy" he responded. His bitch was just holding on to him with her nose turnt up. "Beau, you good?" he asked." I'm excellent!" i said buzzed. He made small talk with Shawn as i danced in my seat looking fine as fuck! I checked my phone until they walked off. He had asked was we dating and being nosy. " Dude want you" Shawn whispered. " I don't blame him, i'm fine as fuck!" i said. Shawn laughed at my conceited ass. My phone chirped confirmation that someone texted me. " Bitch ima rape your slutty ass!" Damn! He tripping i thought as i looked over to their table that was also in VIP. HE WAS STARING..Shit! What the fuck was his problem? He had a bitch with him, fuck that, I'ma do me! I danced with several different niggas and one white boy.

Nobody run me but me. I kept getting disturbing text from him. " You are a Whore! I got a REAL BITCH!! Slutty Whore! The text got more vulgar as the night went on and he got more buzzed. No one noticed his harassment but me. I laughed and accepted drinks from dudes and a couple females sent me a drink. I ignored my phone putting it in my bag. It was after 2 am and i was ready to go home. " Bitch, lets go to the after hour" Zaya said as we got in her whip, Shawn had walked us out and we exchanged digits and i gave him a nice hug and kiss on the cheek. " Bitch lets go" i said not wanting to spoil her fun and plus i was looking too fine to end the night.

21. Carlos, I Can't Do This!

Beautiful: Tomica nasty ass gave Carlos my number! I got a call from a unknown number. "Hello" I said soft and sexy. "What it do, this Los. Ooh i got wet. "Hey Los, what's good" I asked, a lil nervous. "I wanna fuck you and give you money" he said. " Damn" I breathed out dazed. I liked that thug loving. "Los no this doesn't feel right" i said feeling guilty. "Look that nigga got ole girl knocked up so you needs to wise up and fuck wit a real nigga" he dry snitched.

Niggas wasn't shit. "Look foreal foreal, i just wanna talk sexy." he said all sly. "Los what we got to talk about, that's supposed to be your homeboy" i said "Pussy my friend" he laughed. "Look let me take you out and i promise you gonna like me and we gonna fuck" he said thickly. Wow, i loved his confidence. "Let's meet up at a lowkey bar or something" I suggested. "Just come to my place and I'll make something good and healthy" he said. " That's a bet" I agreed.

He gave me directions and we hung up. I was running late and decided to wear some ripped blk jeans, a green tube and some green 4 inch pumps. My hair was in box braids reaching my waist. I got over to his house a half hour late. He had been blowing me up. I got to a nice big house and he was already at the door by the time I walked up. He had on a wife beater and some basketball shorts and house shoes with Nike socks. "Damn girl, I thought you stood me up" he said, hugging as he pulled me in and I hugged him back. "Damn you so fine, i been wanting you for the longest but i knew Lano was tryna fuck" he said honestly. Mhmmm. "What you cook me" I asked."Fish tacos and homemade lemonade" he said proudly. "Carlos, I can't do this" I said, feeling guilty. He held my hand as we walked to a big ass chef kitchen. Nice..the countertops blk marble and matching marble floors..different and unique coloring.

He had set the four chair high table with backed bar stools chairs. I set as he prepared our plates and he sat in front of me fish tacos but instead of taco shells it was a huge leaf of green romaine lettuce and it looked so good. I was smashing and it was so good and the lemonade was fresh and made with organic lemons. I was impressed. He told me he had a baby mama and their son was 3.

He had washed his dope money and bought a couple dolla stores and a few rental properties. "So what do you want from me" I asked. "A good time" he answered. He was so different. We moved to the living area and it was different tones from bronze to chocolate browns. "I like your house and it's so clean" I said. "I pay my sister to come clean twice a week for me" he laughed. His gold eyes were hypnotizing me."Come here" he said, pulling me across the huge couch. I had kicked off my heels as soon as I walked in. He sat me on his erection. "You're so pretty and sexy" he moaned, kissing my neck. "Los we cannnttt" i stuttered. "Shhh, let me make you feel good" he said low as he pushed down my tubetop and released my chocolate orbs.

 I was so fucking sore i thought as i left Los house the next morning. That dude had a huge dick. He made me squirt on his dick multiple times. He made me promise to hang out again real soon. Delano had been calling and texting and now i was nervous as fuck. I hope Carlos kept his damn mouth closed. When i pulled up Lano car was in the driveway. I walked in and he was with his homeboy Steve. "Where the fuck you been" he yelled at me. "At my parents house" I lied. He pulled me in my kitchen. "I swear to God if you fucked another nigga yall both dead" he threatened.

"Ouch, you hurting me" i cried. I was glad Steve was there. "I was at my parents house, i needed a break" i said letting the tears flow. He believed me. "Look, ima be gone until late so don't try to be sneaky and go out, stay your ass at home!" he said. I felt guilty but he had that hoe at the bar pregnant. I was gonna do me. He talked more shit to me but eventually left. I soaked in a hot bath for my pussy soreness. I was exhausted. Carlos was very sexually skilled and I liked how blunt and to the point he was. As I soaked I kept playing in my head over and over how he moaned my name every time he bust. It was so sexy.. I eventually got out and lotioned myself with a chocolate banana moisturizer and laid in my bed naked. I was woken up to Lano fucking me and i always had either gum or breath mint in my mouth even when sleeping so he moaned when he kissed me and tasted sweet mint.

 "Ahhh Beau, fuck! Have my baby" he whispered harshly with choppy breaths. "Lano, don't cum in me" I said. He just bit my neck and then grabbed my ass and grinded in me and I gasped from taking all that thick black meat. Orgasm hit me hard. "Oh oh oh ohhhh, damnnn" I cried as my body was jerking as my pussy rained on his cock as I contracted on his dick over and over as I saw stars. As I came back to reality he was pulling out his semi hard dick. "Don't worry I didn't cum" he grinned.

I felt down there and looked at my fingers and it was thick gooey white matter. "So what's this Delano" I asked. "Your cum, i told you i didn't cum " he said laughing all sly. "Whatever, don't try to get me pregnant, I don't want a baby" I said madly. Now that i was fucking two niggas i had to be real careful, i wasn't trying end up on MAURY..

22. Niggas Be Tricking Hard!

"Beau, I got you something" Carlos texted. "Oh yeah?" i texted back."Come to my house tonight so I can give it to you " he text. " I can slide through at like 8" I texted. " Cool, I got you" he texted. I had to make up an excuse to Delano because he watched my every move. I had only fucked with Carlos that one time. He had given me shopping money that I actually put in my account. I had new clothes and shoes for a couple months. Frfr.. As I got ready I felt slightly dizzy and nauseous. I needed to eat.

 I thought as I slid on a mid thigh mini dress that was a mesh material that was bronze colored and I grabbed my gold clutch and threw on my gold stilettos that criss crossed up my calf. I was planning on fucking Carlos and getting my gift. I Had told Delano I was going out to dinner with my family and movies afterward. He was tying up ends on some business so he was busy and happy I would be with my fam. Lol.

I slid on my black leather rocker jacket and walked to my vehicle. I puffed on a blunt as I cruised to Carlos' crib.

Damn i was a sneaky lil hoe i laughed to myself. I got to Carlos house and he was on the phone with someone as he waved me in after kissing my smooth cheek. "Sis i wanna know who the nigga is that got you spending all your time with when you come in town" he chuckled. I laughed at his brotherly protectiveness. Awww. "How are you doing sexy" he asked after he got off the phone. "Good good" i answered. We made small talk and he gave me a beautiful emerald and diamond gold bracelet. We ate a healthy salad with baked chicken breast and white wine. We took it to his room and he fucked me nice and slow. "Be my woman Beau" he asked as he stroked my delicate pussy. I moaned as he picked up his pace.

Needless to say it was some great sex wit a fine ass nigga! We laughed and I finally agreed to stay the night. I called Delano and acted as if I was buzzed and my cousin was gonna drop me off at home a lil later and he told me he was gonna go to his crib and get some paperwork together and would take me out for breakfast tomorrow.I made sure to park around the block. Cool, I was good for the night.

 We joked around and we heard his front door open and muffled laughing. "That's my crazy sis and her company" he explained. I laughed at the commotions. "Let's crash the party" he grinned. I was in his big tee shirt and his socks."Hell yeah leftovers" i heard the drunken female voice. I giggled as we stepped in the kitchen. I dropped my glass of wine and it hit the tiled floor as me and DELANO made eye contact. Fuck! I was fucking his best friend and he was fucking Carlos sister…

23. Caught Thee Fuck Up Bihh

Delano: I had been kicking it with a female I met a few months ago. She was cool and willing to be outta town pussy. Beau was my main bitch but i had plan b just in case. Her name was Lianna and she was Puerto Rican and sexy as hell. She had come by my detail shop a few months ago and I had come in to bring car cleaning products to my manager/ cousin. I saw her sexy ass sitting there with a sexy red dress on and I gave her my business card letting her know I was the owner.

She also gave me her business card. This weekend she was staying with her brother Carlito. The hotels was booked due to a huge tourist event. Beau was with her family out of town so I was good. I was slick as fuck i laughed to myself.

 I was slowly letting all my hoes go for Beau tight pussy ass. She was a sneaky lil bitch but i still wanted her.

Carlos: I wanted that chocolate bitch to be my bitch. Beautiful was a top notch bitch and I would crown her as my queen. The night I was over her crib wit Tomica, i knew i had to fuck her. I had been crushing on Beau for a long ass time and I hated when Delano said he took her virginity. I asked to Tomica to give my #'s to Beau lowkey. I gave her a couple hunnid to pass the message to Beau. I was out chea handling my business so I could take care of a bad bitch like her. I was 26, 6" nice abs and females loved my light brown complexion and hazel eyes. My baby mama was crazy but I took care of my son who was 3.

My sister's had a key to my crib so whenever they came in town they had a place to stay. My younger sis always came to clean for me. Liana had texted and said her and a guy friend would probably come later on that night. I was talking on the phone when I saw Beau jeep pull up and she walked up in a bikini top and ripped jeans. My dick got hard. "Okay sis i wanna see the nigga you spending all your time with when you in town" i said kissing Beau cheek and she smelled so goddamn good.

Her stuck up ass came in and I hung up with my sister. I fed her and we took it to my bedroom "Los damn you so fine" she said as i ate her pussy. She was moaning and I came up and slid in that tight twat. Oh fuck! She felt like heaven I thought as her pussy squeezed me. "Beau be my woman" I groaned as we both climaxed. We showered and laid back naked and smoked a blunt. We were talking about different shit and I heard laughing. "My sister, I thought. But she wasn't alone tho. "Let's be nosy lil mama" I said , giving her my T-shirt that swallowed her thick but slim figure.

We came down the steps and Beau had her wine sipping as we walked to the kitchen. "Leftovers" I heard Lianna laugh tipsy and her guy friend chuckled.

Beautiful: "Yeahh yeahhh, Los you are so sexyyyy" i moaned as he ate my pussy. He came up and slid his big dick in me. "Be my woman Beau" he said as he slid in and out. His hair was in a ponytail and was coming loose and I grabbed his hair and french kissed him and he groaned loving it. He stroked my pussy real good until we both climaxed.

He hadn't used a condom but he withdrew his dick and jerked off all over my belly and thighs and I loved seeing his dickhead spit out all that white cum as he groaned. "My sister" he said a while later when we heard laughter and noise. He gave me his shirt and I had my wine. I walked in and met eyes with Delano! Fuck, i thought as my wineglass fell and i felt as if the walls was closing in as he went straight for Los. "You fuck nigga!, i knew you wanted my bitch" Delano yelled as him and Los was wrestling in the big kitchen as me and Lianna watched. That hoe came for me and I had to put these hands on her ass. "You nasty slut" she said, pulling my hair. I punched her as we were fighting in her mouth. I felt someone tear us apart and it was Delano. "Get your ass in the car now Bitch" Delano yelled at me as Los held back his sister.

"You black ass hoe, he wants me bitch" Lianna screamed. "Fuck you hoe, but he want me to go home with him bitch" i screamed grabbing my bag. Delano pulled me by my hair to his car. " I'm sorry bae" I said scared. "You a lil hoe Beau, my homeboy" Delano asked mad as he slapped me and then started his car. I was so nervous as he pulled out his pistol and put it on his lap. "Delano im sorry bae, it was only a few times and i was gonna break off things with him tonight anyways" i lied and he was so quiet.

Delano: I was mad as fuck as i fought my homeboy. He was sneaky as fuck. We then ended up pulling Lianna and Beau apart. I pulled Beau out to my car as Lianna taunted us. "That black hoe will never be me" Lianna screamed to me as Los held her. They now looked so much alike I thought as Beau said "Bitch and he's taking me home and leaving you ugly hoe" she yelled back. Damn! Lianna had said she was pregnant but i chose Beautiful over her. I slapped Beau when we got in the car. "You a lil hoe and you gonna see what happens to my bitch when she disloyal" i said taking my heater out of my waistband and setting it on my lap purposely scaring her.

24. Domestic Violence

Beautiful: I begged Delano to just let me explain everything as he drove to the apartment he paid for me. I was so scared as he went off me. "You a fucking young hoe, how long you been fucking my homeboy Beau" he asked pulling into the parking lot. It was a bit cold as I only had on Carlos Tshirt and socks. I sat frozen not wanting to get out. He got out and came around and opened my door.

"Get the fuck out now Slut" he gritted out and his bottom four platinum shining in the moonlight. "Please Lano, please don't beat my ass, I can't take it please" I cried scared. "My parents don't beat me so please" i said so scared. We got in and he immediately slapped me hard. "Bitch i should kill your stupid ass!" he screamed.

He dragged me by my hair to my room. "Fucking wash that nigga scent off you hoe" he said pushing me to the bathroom holding my cheek crying. He ripped the T-shirt off as I whimpered. "You my bitch" he said as I got in the shower and used my expensive body wash Delano had bought me. I prayed that he didn't beat my ass. He was yelling at someone on the phone as I dried off. "Bitch, you were outta town pussy and it wasn't that good" he said laughing. "Tell Los bitch ass, watch his back Ma" he said hanging up. "Lay down" he barked. I laid down naked and he sat fully clothed on the side of the bed. He slowly traced my body slowly. "No woman has cheated on me Beautiful, but you wanna be different huh" and I shook my head no.

"Bae, I didn't mean for it to go that far" I said and he put his finger over my lips to shush me. "Beau, open real wide" he said, caressing my thighs. I opened and felt something cold and looked down, a FUCKING GUN. "Please Delano, I'm sorry, I'll do whatever you want" I said as tears rolled down my face.

He pressed the barrel against my pussy. "I could destroy you in seconds" he said low. "Why Beau, why Los, you like them pretty niggas" he said jealous. "Tomica gave him my number and he said he just wanted to smoke some blunts and it went too far Bae, im sorry, i only want you" i begged needing him to remove the gun. He got on top of me and thrusted his big dick in me. I screamed and he choked me as he fucked me hard. He put the pistol to my head."Bitch make me cum in this pussy, I'ma get your pretty ass pregnant tonight whore" he said.

Delano: "Bitch, you bet not ever give my pussy away, you hear me" I said, choking her ass as I fucked her. I needed her scared to ever disrespect me again. "Ahhh ahhh, I love you Beautifullll" i groaned cumming in her. "Your pretty ass getting pregnant tonight" I said, taking the gun from her temple. I pulled out and asked "Did you and Los use protection?" and she nodded. "Fucking talk bitch" i yelled. "Lano, we used a condom" she said, sitting up against the headboard. She was so pretty and sexy. "Did he make you cum" I asked, needing to know.

"Delano, please let's not talk about him, let's talk about us" she said. Is that the woman you got pregnant" she asked and it shocked me she knew. Fuck!. "Baby it's not mine, I ain't never fucked her raw" I said. "But you beating my ass tho" she said smartly. "Beau don't talk too much, i been real nice considering you fucking my homeboy, that shit embarrassing as fuck" i said mad.

 We cleaned ourselves and I made her ass cook me some breakfast food naked. Her punishment included no clothes for a month when we were alone, no clubbing, no cheating. "So if it's your baby, then what" she asked as she made pancakes. "You gonna be step mommy" I joked. "Bae, i'm so sorry" she said as I watched her ass jiggle as she moved in her stilettos. She was gonna be my woman until i tired of her but i was her first and that kept a nigga coming back. She was a challenge and I loved a challenge. She was young but sneaky so I had to keep an eye on her ass. I am going soft on Beautiful.

25. Losing A Friend

Beautiful: I woke up sore as fuck! I had so many missed texts and calls and voicemails. "Yeah, I'ma be at the crib all day, come through and bring ya lady, we can do the couple thangs bra" i heard Delano say over the phone. I went to my bathroom and brushed my teeth and washed my face. I had a dark ring under my left eye and my pussy was so sore. My whole body ached from fighting Lianna and from Delano manhandling me.

 I called my parents and said I wanted some time off to enroll back in school and our help at the store would love the extra hours. They had no problem with me furthering my education so they said whatever I needed.

 I loved them so much. I brushed my hair in a curly ponytail after putting in some curl defining gel. I hated not being able to wear clothing as punishment. "Come here" I heard Delano say and I hurried and went to him in fear. "Yes bae" I asked sweetly. "I got a few of my people coming through with they ole ladies so i need you to get some drank, snacks for my place" he said. "By what time bae" I asked. "Tonight at about 7, put some makeup over that bruise" he said gruffly. He didn't even apologize for bruising my face. He was a piece of shit! "Get dressed so i can eat, your ass ain't got barely any groceries. Shit, only time the fucking fridge is full is when i put food in there" he said irritated. I stayed quiet as I went to my room to get dressed. Ughhhh, I hate him. I cried inside. He was so fucking mean. I know i fucked up but so did he. He possibly had that stank hoe pregnant. I had so many texts from Carlos. He was begging for me to be with him and he said he wanted to take care of me and shit. Whatever, right now I was just tryna get through the moment with this crazy ass nucca.

I put on some a red cotton jumper that fit my sexy body and some red Forces. "Damn your thick ass gonna have me catch a case" he said slapping my ass making it tremble. He got dressed in a new pair of khakis, some leather black loafers and a black button up. He looked so sexy and his hair was growing out to nice waves and his body was so fine.

"Lets go, im hungry as fuck" he said as i rolled a blunt. I needed it for my nerves. I had put on some expensive concealer to hide my bruise under my eye. My phone rang and it was Zaya. "Hey girl, what's good Bihhh" I said tryna sound happy and normal. "Bihhh where ya ass been, the word is Los and my brother was fighting over your bitch ass" she said. "Hold up bitch, i fucks who i like and what you heard is true hoe" i said hanging up. "My nosy ass sister found out already" Lano asked and i nodded. Zaya was my bitch but she fucked up when she tried to dog check me. Bitch was mad cause she had a crush on Los like every other bitch we knew and yes i was fucking her brother also.

These hoes was some real haters. We made it to the nice breakfast only establishment that Delano knew the owners personally. I order bacon, cheese grits, scrambled eggs and wheat toast and orange juice and no sweetened tea. "Delano, Zaya mad at me" I said as we waited for our food. "Oh fucking well, worry about yo nigga being mad at you" he said texting as usual. "Lano i'm not gonna be the bitch with the nigga with like five hoes. You just gonna have to beat my ass!" i said pissed. It's his fault Zaya was mad at me.

Delano: I hated seeing her bruised but she needed to be scared. She still had a lil attitude with her sexy thick ass. I told her to get dressed to go out to eat breakfast at a friend of mine's nice restaurant who specializes in breakfast food. "Bae , Zaya is mad at me for lying about me and Los messing around, i think she had a crush on him" she told me as we waited on our food. "Don't worry bout that, worry about how i could fuck you up" i said. She smacked her lips. "We're going to meet my family real soon" I said, wanting her acquainted with my moms. Zaya would come around eventually. Lianna would have to get a Dna from me to prove I was her baby daddy. The only bitch my mind was on was Beautiful. I stared as she texted whoever and then she grinned so pretty. "Who the fuck texting you" i said jealous. She showed me her phone and it was her parents holding up the deuces in a selfie. "Dang your mom fine as fuck" i said."Thank you" she smiled. "I wanna meet them Beau" I said.

 Our food came before she could answer. I stared as she ate her food. "Why did you do it Beau" I asked. "Delano please, not here and i'm sorry bae" she said embarrassed.

"You right, let's move on" I said. I was gonna get her lil whorish ass pregnant. I was gonna make her sit the fuck down. We went to my crib and she brought clothes and shoes and she had shit over there already. I had close friends coming over tonight. "Get fucking naked, you still on punishment slut" i said and she mumbled something and i grabbed her hair "Don't make me mad Beau" i said as she nodded as tears formed in her eyes from my tight grip. She was gonna go through hell as my bitch i laughed inwardly

26. Moving Forward

Delano: I had her scared as fuck. She was scared of my threat to her parents. I didn't like the bruise she had from me slapping her but she needed to do what the fuck i said. I was chilling as she went and got some snacks and liquor for my lil get together tonight with my cuz Quita. Me and Qui had always been best friends and her girlfriend was cool as shit. I had Qui and her girl go with Beau lil sneaky ass. They had come by and smoked a couple blunts and talked shit. Qui would beat the breaks off her bitch if she even spoke outta turn.

I had once seen her girl laugh at some nigga joke and Qui beat her ass. She knew to keep her head down and don't say shit. Qui was a gorgeous brown skin woman and her girl was a beautiful light skin woman and they were both 24. Also they both dressed promiscuously and occasionally cuz fucked niggas for money and that's the only time her girl would get loud and act crazy. She was mad and jealous of Qui and she loved her. Actually I was having another cuzin come through and a few homeboys and some ladies and hoes. It was kinda a couple's thang but you always get the stragglers that're single and ready to mingle. "Where the fuck you at" i said when Beau answered her cell. "Bae I'm on my way, you need gas and Qui had me stop and get some smoke" she explained and I heard Qui laughing "Tell cuz we are coming, his ole jealous ass, i ain't gonna take your bitch cuz" Qui laughed. "Fuck Qui!, get your ass here, you got 30 minutes" i said hanging up.

Beautiful: Ughhhh, i didn't want to go with these dike hoes. They seemed like regular pretty girls that had on mini dresses and heels but them hoes was fucking. I had met Qui a few times and she was a boss bitch and she had niggas and hoes.

She always kept a nice crib and new whip. We went to Meijer to get margarita mix and liquor and a few cases of beer. I drove Delano car and more than a few hoes was looking when i got out of his car with Qui and Bria. "Damn they hating you in cuz car" Qui laughed. "Bihhh i know right " i said noticing hoes peeping me. "Bitch if they run up, we all throwing hands" Qui said and I had to laugh because she was about that life and I loved that.

 I actually had a new respect for her knowing she wouldn't let these hoes jump me. We made it back to Lano house and he had music on and he had some guy laying new carpet down in his fully finished basement. "Bae, I'm gonna go change before everybody makes it here" I said kissing his lips. I showered and moisturized my face and soft brown body. I rubbed my hard nipples and moaned as they hardened. I wanted some dick. I was becoming addicted to having orgasms and I loved the way men groaned while they fucked me. I loved that Delano was having this party so i could see more niggas to fantasize about. Plus i loved men wanting to fuck me and eat my pussy.

I had only fucked two dudes but i wanted more dick and different dick. I was planning on going to live-in Detroit with my cousin Pam. The bitch was a stripper and she escorted but i was tryna get away and fuck some niggas wit bread. I had money saved up and I would stay with her to learn the area and get my own lil place and job.

 We had talked several times lately and she lived in the outskirts of Detroit in a nice upscale black area from what she told me. Anyways until then i would deal with this crazy ass negro. And now me and my bihh were beefed out. "Zaya girl, 'i'm sorry i fucked your lil crush but i ain't kissing your ass" i said when she called again talking shit. "Bihhh and you fucking my brother, take several seats Beau" she said. "Bihh, you know i do me tho" i said. We hung up after talking trash. For now I was done wit her.

 I was looking sexy as fuck and Delano was bout to talk shit as usual about how i look like a slut or hoe. Whateva, I would go along with this clown but I was done with his ass too. I came down the stairs and saw the cutest dude ever. He was so fine and thick and sexy. My pussy throbbed at all that masculinity and chocolate.

27. Coming Up With A Plan

A Week Later

Beautiful: I was so tired. Delano had invited a few of his homeboys over and I went to his room and I had to be naked. They were loud and shooting dice $100 a shot . He wanted me to sit in the basement while they did their thang. I had a nice sack of Kush he had got me and I was sipping on Grey Goose and pineapple juice. He hated the way my denim jeans fit. He was in a bad mood all day and he wanted me in his sight 24/7.

When his friends came over I knew to not say shit to them even if they speak to me. "Bae, can I go lay down" I asked, tired of them yelling and talking shit. "Damn let me walk this girl up here" i heard him say to them.

 When we got upstairs to his bedroom he slapped me. "I didn't do nothing" i cried out and tears instantly falling from the pain. "You are such a hoe, all my niggas know bout you and Los bitch ass"he said ripping my shirt off and my big tits sat out proudly, my nipples hard. "Don't Delano, pleassse" i said as he yanked my jeans off and ripped my pretty pink thongs off. He ripped into me "I will fucking kill you if you ever cheat on me again" he said fucking me hard on his bed. He made me kiss him as he raped me and i could hear his friends in the basement and the music playing. "Get pregnant get pregnant" he said as he buried his big black long meat in me flooding my tight pussy with cum. He wiped off his dick with my torn crop top and said "You Better not get on any of that social media bullshit" he said.

I was sniffling still and he yelled "Do you fucking hear me" i jumped and nodded and said "Yes Delano". He walked out slamming the door closed. I was so tired of his bullshit i thought as i took a relaxing bath. I would get revenge on him before i left town and went to Detroit, Mi. I gave myself 2 months to get the fuck outta dodge.

I had been sweeting my parents to the idea of me leaving to pursue my career in Detroit. They were totally against it at first but they would always have my back so i would never fall off. I wanted to fuck Delano cuz, Tone. He was so fine and sexy. He was down in the basement also and that's why I wanted to leave from down there. I couldn't look at him like I wanted to and I felt Delano eyes on me.

I had made shrimp scampi and brussel sprouts for dinner. "Yo lil stuck up ass can cook, this shit good" he said loving my food. I had some sweet white wine to go with dinner. He was going to miss my ass when I left him. He took a shower and I rubbed cocoa butter all over him and he had beautiful flawless dark skin and his sexy body made me horny as his big black dick got hard as I caressed the lotion into his skin.

"Suck it" he said thickly. He didn't have to say it twice. I needed the experience anyways I thought as I sucked his big dickhead. "Damnnnn Beau" he groaned. I licked up and down his shaft and his dick leaked pre cum. "Delano, i love you" I said , stroking up and down his dick while sucking his dickhead. "Oh fuck! Beautiful, I love you" he said as I almost choked on the huge amount of semen in my throat as he deepthroated me gripping my hair.

 I loved the power of making a thug ass nigga cum crying out my Full name. Lmao. I cleaned his cum on his dick, balls and muscular thighs. "We going to my moms this weekend" he said in my ear. I rolled my eyes. Great!, all i needed, a hating ass old bitch mad because i had her son pussy whipped i thought as we fell asleep.

That weekend

Beautiful: "Don't fucking be disrespectful and shit around my moms" he said as we rode the 267 miles to where his mom lived. He had sisters and brothers in the small town he was from. This was definitely gonna be an interesting weekend. I was trying to enjoy my weekend and I had some new clothes I had packed that were cute. I had my hair in box braids so i didn't have to mess with it while at his moms house. New adventures is how I looked at it. He told me to act mature and say I was 26.

I wondered how this shit was gonna play out as we pulled up to a huge ranch style home and several expensive vehicles were in the long driveway. "Ahh man, I forgot a few of my cousins are visiting" Delano said excitedly. I was hoping it was niggas cause i didn't like too many hoes, they always hated on me. He grabbed our luggage with the wheels. He opened the door without knocking and I entered the richly decorated home and loved the lemon wax on the beautiful wood floors that smelled so light and refreshing. "Ma, where are you at" he said grinning, seeing food wrapped in foil containers and I smelled BBQ smoke. We walked through the family room and then the kitchen which led to the back yard with the swimming pool and two grills going. There were lots of ppl back there. "Damn, I forgot the family reunion is this weekend" he said. "Baby we both need to enjoy ourselves" i said seeing a gang of niggas with they shirts off. We walked out to the entertaining strangers. Shit! I was ready to have some and mingle.

28.Riding His FACE..

Beau: Ugghh, I saw Zaya and we didn't speak but I was determined to get buzzed and have fun. They older brother Kian and his girlfriend was there and her name was Kenya and she was cool as hell. "Girl, so how do you like DeLano?" Kenya asked. "He is cool and he is really nice to me" I lied. She laughed hard as fuck from my lil skit. "Chile please, Kian and DeLano is some crazy ass niggas" she said looking around as she whispered. "Yeah, Delano is something different" I said.

"Girl, i see the black eye" she said, lifting her Gucci sunglasses and revealing a black eye also. Omg! "Girl you how old" Kenya asked. "Im 20 but Delano told me to say im 26" i confessed to this hoe i barely knew but she seemed cool as fuck. We was in the kitchen making a drank and she rolled up some purple as i sipped my drink.

 I found out her and Kian had been together for almost two years. When you looked at us, we could be family. She was almost the same chocolate skin tone but she had gold eyes where mines was a really dark green. Got em from my grandma. "Yeah Kian is a good guy but too jealous Beau" she said as we chatted. "Same wit Delano but i did fuck his friend Carlos" i said ashamed. She laughed "Good for Delano dog ass, he dog them hoes" and i had to laugh. Zaya spoke to Kenya and they hugged. "That's my bihh but she mad cause i didn't tell her about me and Delano or Los" i said. "Yeah them niggas done ran through all her friends seem like" Kenya said sipping her drink through the straw. I liked her swag of a bad bitch, I could definitely relate to her.

Delano and Kian walked over and they both was aggressive as fuck with us. "Yall plotting" Kian said, half serious/ half joking. "Bae we are just talking about clothes and hair and that new mall" Kenya said sweetly. "Bae, can i go with her to that new mall tomorrow" I asked Delano. "Mannn, all you want is money and weed" he said annoyed. Kian laughed "Nigga, i swear that's all Kenya want" and Delano laughed at that giving him dap.

 The big shuttle buses they rented picked up the out of town people to take them to the hotel so they could get ready for other activities. I then saw Tone fine ass and he was with a different white girl this time. Okay I see what type he was, I thought to myself. I was gonna see how cool Kenya really was. I said coming up with a plan. "He is so fine but he loves white girls" Kenya said. I laughed and said "I just wanna ride his face". "Girl, that makes two of us" she smirked. "I need to get him alone so I can ride on his face" I said seriously. "Yall here all weekend" she asked and I nodded. "I should be able to help you out" she said. I flirted low key with Tone and he kept licking those juicy lips and I knew he wanted to eat my pussy. I hoped Kenya was a legit type bitch. "Tomorrow night we gonna give Tone a lifetime of memories" she smiled prettily.

Delano mom was a sweet lady as usual and we got a beautiful decorated guest room. "You good sexy" Delano asked, kissing me. I nodded yeah. "I was talking shit, I'ma give you money to go shopping with Kenya, she is a good girl" Delano said and I laughed inside at that. "Thank you bae" i said kissing his thick lips standing on my tip toes as i had kicked off my stilettos.

He fucked me after we showered and I really enjoyed the way he moaned my name as he fucked me slow. I had an amazing orgasm on his thick dick throbbing in me as he released his kids in me.

I fell asleep before he took out his dick and I remembered him saying "You better not ever cheat on me again" as I fell asleep exhausted.

THE NEXT DAY Beau

"Ooh these french toast is soooo good" I moaned as the food just melted in my mouth. We and all the guests were served a catered buffet breakfast Delano mom paid for. It was amazing food and customer service and I asked for a business card. Kenya smoked a blunt before we ate so I had the munchies and smashed the food. "Let's go do laps around the house in a few hours" I suggested. "Yes, I gotta stay in shape, I love clothes" Kenya said.

I was glad I had brought several workout clothing items and shoes. "Girl, I hear tonite that Delano and Kian are going to the strip club" Kenya said as we walked briskly before starting a jog. "Hmm, so how do I get sexy ass Tone alone" I asked. "Girl i told him discreetly to meet me in the library tonight by himself" she explained.

I laughed at her fast work. " Yasss bitch yasss" I said clapping as she laughed."Let's jog those calories off from all that fat ass food we ate" Kenya said and we jogged for at least 30 minutes.

Hmmm, Delano while you at the strip club, I'ma ride Tone face..lolzzzzzzi thought. "Beautiful, i'm going out with the guys so hang out with Kenya and i'll be back around 12" he said putting on his gold chain with the diamond and gold Jesus piece. He was looking so sexy. "Yeah don't fuck no bitches either" i said slightly jealous. It had been busy all day with some of the family reunion activities was at Delano mons house. I enjoyed the different attractive family members and they was nice people. "Have fun" I said , kissing him as he and Kian and a few other cousins walked out and got in a Delano Camaro and Kian Lincoln truck.

They was headed to the titty bar. "Meet us down in the library for drinks" Kenya texted. I had went and changed to a mini dress and avoided his moms prying nosy ass. I had no panties or bra on. Easy access. I knocked lightly and the door opened and it was Tone and John that was Tone homeboy that had came over to Delanos recently. Hmmm, these niggas wasn't shit. I saw that Kenya titties and ass was on display as well.

I walked in and Kenya locked the door to the barely used library that was small but had nice firm couches and end tables of the finest wood and several huge bookcases. Two desk with laptops and a huge flatscreen mounted on the wall. "So gentleman we ain't got all night" Kenya said collecting money from both niggas "I got you bitch" she said putting the money in her bag. I sat on Tone lap and he grabbed my ass and said "Good, no panties" as i grinded in his dick. He was so fine and i loved he had a woman. "I.wanna ride.your.face Tone" i said and he slid down the couch and said "I love eating pussy and ass". I sat on his face and rode his thick tongue as he caressed my breast. Kenya and John was already fucking and moaning. It was a crazy experience as he ate my ass as i bent over the couch. "Oh my God!" i cried as he finger fucked my pussy as he ate my ass. He put on a condom and fucked me so good with his medium sized dick.

He groaned as i told him how good he made me cum "Fuck fuck, your pussy so tight" as he pumped fast cumming in the condom. Needless to say we left them niggas drained and we split the $1200 they had gave Kenya. I felt like a high priced hoe when she said to take a hot bath to tighten up my pussy so Delano wouldn't think anything. I giggled as I bathed when Delano came through the door drunk asf demanding pussy.

 I rode his drunk dick and when he came I tried to get off and he held me down holding my waist. "Delanoooo stopp" i said mad. He knew I didn't want a baby right now. I had to make sure to get some plan b pills tomorrow. I thought about it falling asleep.

29. Cheating Ass!

Delano: Me and a few of my niggas went to the titty bar that i frequent when i was in town. Tone wasn't feeling good so he was gonna be up under that sickly looking white hoe he brought with him. That nigga loved them white girls.lol.

 I had $300 in $1 bills to make it rain on a bad bitch. The music was blasting and hoes was fucking the stripper poles for dollas. I saw a bad redbone bitch that was making that ass clap. Shit, Beautiful was the first dark skin chick i was in a relationship with and she had the most dog ass bitch attitude. Stuck up bitch!

I was always attracted to dark skin women but they seemed to not be feeling me so i dealt with hoes that wanted me which tended to be light skin or non black. Anyways I wanted some brains tonight from that yellow hoe. " Aye tell her i got a hundred for some dances" i told the almost naked waitress. I tipped her 10 bucks and she grinned and walked over to the dancer and pointed to me. The niggas that came with me was doing them and the stripper hoes came to our table because they knew niggas wit money. Her sexy ass walked over jiggling titties and ass. My dick got hard asf. "Wassup baby" she grinned and her teeth were kinda bucked and she had some acne but she would do. "Dance" I demanded. She slid on my lap and twerked and grinded on me. "Show me how you fuck" i said after a few minutes.

She was sweating for them dollas. "Damnnn i wanna fuck you, you so sexy" she said in my ear over the blasting music. I grinned showing my bottom grill. She moaned knowing I had cake. "Come to the back" she said, taking my hand.

I followed with my drank and money. We did a couple lines of Coke and I let her worship my dick and afterwards I gave her a hundred dollar bill. She grinned and wanted my number which I gave her. I got back to my mom house and showered and slid in bed naked with Beau "You smell so good baby" she said as I rode that pussy hard and sucked her big titties as they bounced. I slid my hands under her and gripped that ass as i fucked her "Fuck.me.back" i said loving her cries of extasy. "I love you Beautiful" i said cumming in her tight cat. "You're gonna be my baby mama so get used to it" I said after I pulled her to me.

The next day(Sat)

"Let's go down for breakfast" he commanded after we showered together. I had on a cute short sundress that was green matching my eyes and tan pumps and a tan leather Gucci bag. I saw Tone and avoided his eyes. "Good morning hun" Delano mom said to me."Yes ma'am good morning" i said respectfully. She acted as if her sons were everything even though she heard how they talked to us and saw how they treated us and she said nothing.

 "Hey girl" Kenya said, sitting across from me at the huge 20 chair table. I smiled at my new friend. "Hey" I said as Delano was chopping it up with Tone and his brother. "You missed out my nigga" Delano grinned looking so fucking sexy i thought. "I heard" Tone laughed sitting next to his loud girlfriend who was tryna be down with us black women a lil too hard. I wasn't prejudice but i hated when non blk ppl talked or thought they talked like us and she sounded and looked a mess.

 Oh well, i had fucked her man and he ate my ass. Lmao. "I need money" i said later as i dressed in jeans tee shirt and some shell toe Adidas matching my cropped Adidas tee. "All you want is money and weed" he complained. "And all you want is to rape me and talk shit, even exchange" i said smartly. "Aye don't get that ass beat" he warned. I kissed him and me and Kenya left to do some shopping. Zaya had left i guess this morning. Good, i wasn't tryna fuck wit her anyways now that she knew I was fucking her brother. "Bitch, we gonna make a pit stop and let my nigga Ro smoke us out before we shop" Kenya laughed as she drove her man car. "Bihhh i fucks wit you" i laughed loving the way she operated...Yasssss, she was a dog ass bitch like ME..

30. Delano, Control Your HOES

A Few Weeks Later

Beautiful: I met her dude when had we stopped by her homeboy Ro house and she had met him at the mall and she fucked him from time to time and he gave her money and weed.

She was a sneaky hoe and i was learning tips and tricks from her. Ro was a mixed dude of blk and white and he was fine as hell with dreads to his shoulders. It was a gang of niggas and they was cool and the hoes there was hating on me and Kenya.

They smoked some A1 weed with us and I took Antuan number and we left and went to the mall. "Girl, i just had a abortion by Ro ass, he kept fucking cumming in me and i got pregnant but me and Kian don't use rubbers so i didn't know who was the daddy" she said and we both laughed. I would never get in that position I thought to myself. "How far along was you" I asked. "I was like 6 weeks" she said, pulling up to the mall. We shopped at different stores but I had enough clothing, I wanted sexy ass lingerie. When I entertained my guests when I got a place in Detroit, I would only wear lingerie for my male guests. I was doing me and I could care less if I was being a whore, it was my life. I was still getting paid as if I was working because I was taking my month of vacation pay from my parents so that was stacking up in my account.

The money Delano gave me went to my account also and I was close to 20 racks so I would have a good start when I did my big move. We got back with tons of bags from shopping and I saw Tone and I could tell he was tryna see what's up but he was old news.

I had just wanted to fuck him and i did, moving on. "We are leaving early tomorrow so pack your shit" Delano said, hitting the blunt which he rarely did but he did lines of Coke here and there. Delano fam was having one last cook out before we left. I had a ball regardless of Delano being jealous and I noticed like 4 hoes came over and they weren't family and I wasn't feeling them hoes. "Gurllll, that's Delano ex Chara" Kenya said in my ear.

She pointed to the blasian looking bitch and she was cute but she didn't have shit on me. I then saw the hoe walk over to Delano as he kicked it with a few male cousins. I was gonna see how he handled this hoe before I stepped in. "Hey Lano" she said tryna hug him and he shook her hand looking around to see if I was looking and I was. I Walked over sexy as fuck and said "you are" as he hugged me from behind aer kissing me. "Lil gurl if you don't- i interjected "No bitch, this my nigga and you being disrespectful to a real bitch so back the fuck up, don't let this pretty face and body deceive you" i said. The hoe was scared "Girl don't nobody want Lano, i was just saying hi" she said. "I love him and want him" I said. He laughed as she walked away. "Control your hoes and how was the titty bar, i overheard one of ya cousins saying a bitch sucked ya dick in the room in the back" i said smiling fakely for our audience. He laughed "Your young ass something else" he said wanting to fuck me. "Come here" he said, pulling me inside the house.

 We got to our room and he fucked my brains out. I did kinda like his mean aggressive ass tho.

Delano: I calmed Beau lil sexy ass down after my ex tried to hug me. Beau checked her ass. That shit was so sexy as she checked that hoe. "Control your hoes, and how was the titty bar" she asked. I laughed "Come here" i said pulling her to our room "You got me hard as fuck, sexy ass" i said kissing her and grabbing that fat ass.

 "I don't want no pussy but yours sexy" i said kissing her neck and she smelled so good. I stripped her down and myself and I fucked her hard and good as she screamed"Bae bae it yours, i love you" . "I love you too" I groaned in her ear. I wanted her to be my baby mother. She was young but she was making me so on her. After I made her cum "Pack tonight cause we are leaving early in the morning" i reminded her and she nodded. We had a good time now back to business.

31. Bitch I'm Pregnant!

 Beautiful: "Bihhh, you gotta come and visit" I said to Kenya. She laughed and said" Kian said we were moving close to yall in a few months or sooner". "Girl im tryna be go to Detroit, Mi by then so I'm stacking my chips" I said. This bitch was cool as fuck and she knew ballers too. "Girl, I need you to come visit me and I can't talk over the phone" I panicked whispering to Kenya. Shit shit shit!

I done fucked up. I thought I was nervous hitting the blunt hard. Damn! I needed someone to talk to so badly I thought sadly. Delano walked in my apartment using his key. We had been back from his moms for about a week and everything was going good and he said he forgave me and we were going horseback riding at his uncle's ranch in the country. I was so excited for that. I loved how sweet he was most of the time but i could tell he still had hoes so i was still planning my getaway.

 I confronted his ass one night a few nights ago when we had just finished doing it, his phone rang "Lano, its after one, who the fuck is that?" i asked. "Beau i told that dumb hoe it's over" he said talking bout Lianna. She had been stalking him and leaving crazy messages. Los had tried to contact me over and over also. I wasn't ready to talk to him yet. Kenya and Kian were coming up this weekend and I was so happy, I needed a friend's advice and I felt like Kenya was my long lost sister.

I was tryna get her to go to Detroit with me. I had told her "Gurlll you can bank doing box braids twists and all the hair braiding you do" i said. "Girl when yall left Kian beat my ass because his mom said she couldn't find me all night when they went to the titty bar" she said. "The fuck! Bihhh come with me" i said. "Don't talk too much over the phone because our lines could be tapped by dem crazy muthafuckas" she said paranoid. But I was a whole week late on my period. I had never been late. I had fucked Los, Delano and Tone. Tone used a condom but that wasn't 100 percent. Los didn't use a condom 1 time. I was so scared. Delano never uses a condom.

I went and visited my parents and they spoiled me as usual for things for my apartment and gave me gas cards. I told them my plans and they wasn't happy but they wanted me happy. I loved them so very much. They was so cute together always cuddling and kissing. Relationship Goals! "Beau you ready" he asked as I pulled my hair in a big curly coily ponytail to the back after laying my edges. "Yeah give me a few minutes" i said. "Hurry the fuck up, im hungry" he said. "Okay dang" I said annoyed. I felt my hair being grabbed "Owwww" i cried out. "I saw Los ass today, I knocked his ass out" he said. "Bae, please it hurts" I said knowing I was gonna have a headache later.

 He pushed me away from him hard. "Hurry the fuck up or you getting your ass beat" he said meanly leaving out the room. I was crying after he left the room. He was so mean! I thought as i put on stretchy jeans, a red tee shirt and red on red forces and i was bringing some riding boots. I walked down and he said "Tight ass fucking jeans, you got a whore shaped body. Only hoes clothing fit slutty like yours do" he said viciously.

I ignored him, knowing he was fishing for an argument. He did a few lines of Coke as I got ready. We got to his car and he opened my door for me and got in the driver's seat. "Beau, I'm sorry but I'm still fucked up over you and Los" he said starting the car after kissing me. "It's all good" I said, not wanting to trigger him and he grinned looking so sexy with his bottom four platinum teeth blinging. "Your lil stuck up ass gonna make me catch a case" he said pulling off. "So is you going back to work or what, you got too much free time or you can work for me as a lil assistant" he said. "No, I don't wanna work for your mean ass and I'm actually looking for something, I'm getting vacation time as of now" I said sipping my drink I made before we left.

 He wanted to watch my every move. Uggghh, i was gonna have an abortion. I didn't want his mean controlling ass my baby daddy. I wouldn't be able to do shit. We pulled up to a huge well kept ranch on 55 acres. There were horses, cows, pigs, chickens, goats etc... I was excited until someone ran out to Delano hugging him and he was just standing there awkward. "Oh im sorry, im his school friend Trina" the Bi racial female said. "Hey" I said dryly. Bitch wanted my nigga.

"She is with my cousin before you trip" Delano said "Hey baby, I'm uncle Lee, now you eat hear?" he said, winking at me. I felt instantly better when i seen some niggas and hoes around Delano age out there playing horseshoe which was a southern game(google it). I was gonna get buzzed and enjoy myself and make all the men wanna fuck me i thought. Payback is a bitch Delano. I was gonna abort his child and fuck who i wanted i thought sipping my drank as Delano introduced new faces. "Hey y'all, this my lady Beautiful " said introducing me.

32. My Bihhh Visiting

Beau: "Girllll im so happy you here" i said hugging her. The bitch lip was swollen and she had a small cut under her right eye. "Come to my room" I said , seeing her sad expression. Delano and Kian was laughing talking shit. "Beautiful, see what's playing at the movies" Delano yelled as they headed down in his man cave" the basement".

Delano had just threaten to beat my ass because one of his homeboys said me and Los was still fucking. " Bihhh, i'm pregnant and I don't want Delano baby in me but i don't know if its Lano, Los or Tone baby Ken" i whined to her. "Gurllll you better get a abortion, i done had two.

Kian's best friend Cecil had gotten me pregnant last year and the girl that nucca was dropping a lot of money on me. It was so hard to keep him from telling Kian" she said. "What happened, he just went away" i asked nosy. "Naw the feds got his ass and he is doing 10 years for food stamp fraud.

They caught him with like hundreds of ebt cards " Kenya said. "Gurl it was some fine ass nucca at they uncle Lee farm" i said googling abortion clinics. "Ummm schedule it while i'm here and i'll go with you" Kenya said. "It should be simple and bitch get you some plan b" she laughed. "Thank you bestie." I said. I found a nearby clinic and scheduled for Monday, I was gonna enjoy my weekend. We dressed alike in booty shorts and half tees. It was fun fucking brothers that had money and they was fine as hell. We laughed about how we was gonna fuck some of their friends too. "Bae let me roll up before we leave" I said as me and Kenya sipped some Henny and coke.

"Slow down with all that drinking too, your ass prolley pregnant as fuck" Delano warned me. Fuck him i thought as i rolled up two fat blunts. We were going to drive thru. "Let's change into dresses so they can finger us" I suggested and Kenya agreed as we went up and changed our shorts for mini skirts, nothing underneath.

We grabbed our bags and ran out to our niggas flashy cars. We made it and got side by side parking spots. "Its busy as fuck out here" Delano said. "What you want Sexy" he asked me. "Popcorn and regular m&m's and a coke for my Henny" I said. Him and Kian walked over to the concession stand before the movie started. Kenya came over and sat in the driver seat. She lit the blunt "Girll this some fire". We smoked and she went back to Kian whip. "Bae nooo" i said, pushing his hand away from under my mini. "Let me just feel you damnn, you know you got me pussy whipped" he groaned kissing my neck. "Lanooooo, oooh bae no" I said as he lifted my half tee over my big titties and suckled my nipples that were hard and achy. He laid back my seat. "Open for me, please sexy" he said and he looked so needy and cute. I opened my thick thighs and he plunged two big fingers in me as his thumb caressed my swollen clit. "Yea yeaaaaa" i cried out low fucking his fingers. "I would love to cum in this wet pussy, cum for a real nigga" he said as i tightened up on his fingers as i orgasmed hard seeing stars" I love you i love you Lanooo" i cried out.

He withdrew his fingers sucking off my cum. "You good" I asked, seeing him trying to adjust his erection. "Yea im good" he said with an attitude. "Let me suck it" I said, unzipping his joggers. Ooh he smelled fresh and clean as i sucked his dick head as he groaned.

 I wanted him to fall for me completely so i sucked him off real nice as i massaged his hairy black balls. "Its gonna cum Beau" he warned me and I purposely suckled his dickhead as he jerked crying out my name. I slurped all his cum down my throat greedily loving this power of making him weak and in love.. We made it home and I ordered pizza after me and Delano showered. Kenya and Kian stayed in Delano guestroom across the hall from us and yes we heard Kian take the pussy that night. He had said she was still taking birth control when he had forbidden her to take them. My plan to leave was slowly coming together. I thought as Delano fucked me slowly" I love you Beautiful, i love you" he groaned cumming in me....

33. Filler

Beau: It had been three weeks since my abortion. I was so lucky because the days it took to heal was around the time I had a period every month and Delano didn't suspect anything. Being a hoe was fun. I thought about shopping at the Mall. Delano had given me his black unlimited . Kenya had gone with me before her and Kian left. I was so happy they were moving near us soon. I was hoping Kenya would go to Detroit with me.

We could be roommates and get these nuccas money. Me and her was on the same page as far as fucking these niggas and getting money. I figured i was a sexy fine ass bitch and if a nigga wanted to fuck me, he had to pay nicely. It was only a fair exchange to me.

I had been putting money away like crazy and i would be going to Detroit with a nice new wardrobe so i could stunt on dem hoes. I was so tired of bitches hating on me and that's why i was so cold hearted. I was gonna fuck bitches husbands and boyfriend's. I didn't give a fuck about being nice. I wanted money and big dicks and tongue every night. I could truly enjoy myself when I moved out of town. I would entertain men in lingerie only. I was gonna live my life and eventually get married and have a few brats. I wasn't tryna rush that shit though. I was gonna settle down when I was around 30 or so. I was making small arrangements to move unbeknownst to Delano.

 Delano had been taking me out to nice dinners and hanging out on the weekends but I was so over him. I wasn't tryna settle down in any way. He wanted me to be wifey and shit. Tone had tried to hook up with me but I declined. I would let his white girl have him. Lolzzzz. He wanted me to ride his face again. Niggas loved hoes! My mom raised me as a good girl but I needed to do me. I was a little over a month due to moving and I was so excited.

I wanted to see how them Midwest niggas did it. I was a southern girl so I knew they were gonna love my thick chocolate ass. I needed to find sponsors immediately when I got there, I wasn't tryna be broke, ya know. "Get dressed, we're going to the club" Delano said around 7pm on a Saturday. "I thought we were chilling" I said, not wanting to go out with his jealous ass. "Bae you go, i'll be here waiting on you" i said lighting the blunt. "All you do is smoke, fuck and dress like a slut, get fucking dressed!" he yelled. "Ughhh" I pouted walking to my closet. He walked in behind me. "Aye check that lil bitch attitude, plenty of hoes would love your position as my woman" he said as i looked through new clothes and shoes. I readied myself for this long ass annoying night.

I looked on Facebook and saw it was Delano homeboy Juju birthday bash. He was turning 27. That nucca was sexy as fuck too. He owned some properties and shit doing it big from what i heard. Okay we would be VIP im sure. "Come here Beau" Delano yelled. I walked downstairs and said, `` Yes bae" I asked sweetly. "Be on your best behavior tonight, i don't want no bullshit, this a money situation as well as pleasure" he said and i nodded yes. He kissed me. He had just got a fresh cut and I said how sexy he looked. "You a slick lil bitch" he grinned loving the compliment. Too bad i would be leaving soon i thought. He wasn't that bad as long as he knew my every move.

I got dressed and you know i was sexy as fuck! I smoked a blunt to the head and had a couple shots of vodka. Bitch! I was ready to have a great time. "Damn you got me hard as fuck, ima ride that pussy real good tonight" he said tightly with sexual lust as he held my car door open. I grinned prettily knowing he was pussy whipped. We got to the club and parked in valet. I was dressed for the upscale club in my stretchy catsuit and stilettos. I was buzzed up so I was not so uptight. I swear I spotted Lianna bitch ass. I wasn't sure but it sure looked like that hoe. "I just saw that hoe Lianna" Delano whispered in my ear. I nodded. We headed up to VIP.

It was mirrors, comfy couches, booths with padding, flat screens on all four walls which was huge playing porn. Damnnnnn they were doing it big. This nigga had some bread renting out the whole VIP area. I kept an eye out for his so-called pregnant side hoe. She would still harass us and she just hated that we were still together. She had just sent me an ultrasound pic and I wondered how she got my number.

Delano had no idea and I could tell he really didn't know by his expression. We sat in VIP and when I had to pee, Delano walked right behind me as if my bodyguard and I loved that shit. "Bitch look nasty as fuck in that shit" i heard as i came out the bathroom and Delano was waiting for me.

I kissed him on the lips as I saw the comment came from Lianna stank ass. She laughed and said "I enjoyed that quickie last night baby daddy" she said to Delano and he was silent as we continued to walk. "Bitch ya nigga still fucking me and he gonna take care of his son bitch" I turned and said "Bitch he gonna sign over his rights too, right Lano" i asked his ass. He nodded and said "She ain't shit, lets go". I knew then she was telling the bold face truth. He was still fucking that hoe. Okay, MY TURN BIHHHH

34. Payback Muthafucka!

 Beau "Yeah yeahhhhh" i moaned as his big dick was hitting my spot. He had been wanting to fuck me and shit, why not?. "Damnnn your pussy so wet and tightttt" he groaned. He was high as fuck off Extasy. I had popped a half and I swear this nucca was looking like a black GOD. Everything was so beautiful right now as he fucked me so good. I was so sensitized all over, everything felt so good. Needless to say Quanny fucked me so good and several times. I hoped Delano find out about it because i was leaving in two weeks bihhh.

My cousin Pamela told me to come on and leave Delano disrespectful cheating ass. "Cuz i got you baby, it's plenty of niggas that gonna want to wife you and i know a lot of niggas around this bitch" she laughed. My cousin Pam was a stripper/ hustler/ government assistance getting hoe. But I loved her so much. She had moved to Detroit Like five years ago and we were close before she left and every time she visited we linked up. I loved her son Kavari. He was a cutie and very respectable. She had him in the summers and on holidays, his wealthy white daddy had him the rest of the year. Anyways I showered and kissed Quanny bye and we made plans to hang out again before I left. My girl Kenya and Kian were settling in their upscale 3 bedroom apt a few miles from us. I was still buzzing on Ecstasy but I was good enough to get home. I called Lano "Bae, where are you at" I asked when he answered. "Getting money sexy" he said and I heard some hoe call out his name."Who da fuck dat bitch is" i asked.

"Shit nobody, she is a lil assistant i hired" and i snapped" Im done Lano! And i know you still fucking Lianna stank ass" i screamed hanging up. He called back several times and then texted me. "Beau I swear I ain't cheating, im a couple hours away, be your ass at the house hoe" I went home and laughed because i was leaving his ass soon.

"Bihh come over and smoke, Quan gave me some fire ass weed" I bragged.

He had gave me a few hundred too" i said."Girl that crazy nucca" Kenya asked laughing. "Bihh yea, he cool tho and the nigga made me cum like three times" i laughed also. I had took her over Quanny house and he had a house full of niggas and they blew so many blunts with us as we was supposed to be getting our nails done. Kenya was hollering at Quan cuz Leek. Maleek was a fine dark skin dude that was so sexy and fine with a nice body. " Bih im leaving in two weeks, leave with me" i told Kenya. Kian was just beating her ass and raping her all the time at this point. I really wanted her to come with me and be happy and free and the hoe she wanted to be.

Delano: "Bitch shut the fuck up" i whispered to Lianna. I had been fucking with her still but she had a big fucking mouth. I loved Beautiful but i also had feelings for Lianna. Los had seen me at her house and we had words and for her sake since she was pregnant we squashed the beef. I was praying that hoe ass nigga didn't get the memo to Beautiful. "I love you Baby daddy" Lianna said as her cuz Leena gave me the eye when Lianna back was turned. I was gonna get that pussy in due time. "Aye i'm about to leave" i said standing up. "Papi, I miss you and I need you here with our baby" she said, tears now falling. I knew what she needed.

 I picked her up as Leena watched in jealousy. "I'm about to put ya cuz to sleep, she cant have no company" i grinned as Lianna giggled. " I lovvvvve youuuu" she moaned as i dug that pussy out. "You gonna be here for daddy" I asked about to cum. "Yeahhh yeahh daddyyyy" she cried out cumming hard on my dick. " I love you too" I said , kissing her. I left her some money and hit the highway. "Hello" Beau said, sounding sleepy. "Bitch you better be in my bed naked" I said. "Whateva" she said, hanging up. I loved her lil chocolate ass i thought going 90 mph on the deserted highway.

Beau: I woke up to Delano kissing me. "Go back to ya hoe Lano" i said turning my head from him. "Don't start, i been getting money for you all day" he said, sliding inside me. " Lanooo noo" I protested but he continued to thrust in and out of me. Ughhhh i couldn't wait to leave this no good ass nigga!

35. Bihhhh, THAT PART

Delano " Ahh ahhhh fuck fuck" i groaned as she sucked my hairy balls and then licked my asshole. Oh fuck! Lianna was a nasty lil bitch i thought as she continued to tongue my asshole and then she jerked my big black dick. "Fuckkk, Damnnnnn " i grunted in ecstasy. She had come into town so I fucked her in the upscale hotel. She was a freaky lil pregnant hoe and now i had her turning tricks with a few niggas.

She wanted me and i wanted MONEY. She then sucked on my thick black pipe, deep throating and all. I jerked my dick all over them big yellow titties and wet thick pink lips. She was a nasty bitch! I liked Fucking her, she was so nasty in bed. But Beautiful was my Bae and she was gonna be my baby mother and wifey .

I got up and showered. I was taking Beau to dinner and movies tonight. "Papi, you say you love me but you don't! You want that black hoe!" she cried naked. I pulled her in the shower with me. I felt annoyed with the complaints but for her to continue to bring me the escorting money I had to play nice. "Lianna, i love you and my baby but we need this money to invest in my business." i said kissing her lips softly. "What about the niggas i fuck that cum in me Delano?, Kyle said you told him he could cum in me for an extra thousand dollars" she said as if grossed out. Kyle had said she had multiple orgasms when him and his girlfriend fucked her using vibrators, butt plugs, nipple clamps and so on.

They had her recorded also which I would make copies and sell on the low. I couldn't wife someone so slutty and she had such low self esteem to fuck various men and women while being pregnant to show me loyalty. She was lost cause. She was Los' half sister . He looked more black and she Hispanic. She also thought i didn't love her if once in a while i didn't give her a fat lip or black eye. She loved wearing a black eye from me proudly. I used her low self esteem to my advantage.

"Look, we are close to the prize for a great future for Jr." I said rubbing her big hard tummy. She ate that shit up! Beau called and I made the shhh signal with my finger to my lips. Lianna rolled her eyes mad. " Bring me some food, i'm hungry" Beautiful demanded. "Okay lovely, i'm there in 15 minutes, remember we are going out" i reminded her. "Yeah and you're supposed to be giving me shopping money" she said. "Whateva on my way!" i said hanging up. " You give her ass everything and me just cock" Lianna cried as usual. She passed me $5000 and I was out. I stopped and got Beau some Cigarillos and Henny and coke. I saw Quanny crazy ass! "What up doe" I said to him. "Shiddd tell Beautiful i said what's up" he smirked. "Fuq you mean nigga?" i said offended. "Nigga i said what i said!" he said stepping up and i felt my adrenaline rushing with rage. "Aye Nigga you- and i gave him a right to his jaw and Quan ole bitch ass was out. The store owner was like I've seen dude with a bad ass chocolate bitch a few times, he called her Beau" the messy old man said. I left without getting my change. Beautiful was in deep shit.

 Beautiful: "Bitch he just left from fucking me, haha" Lianna texted me. I ignored it like the other 100 texts from her pathetic life. I heard the door slam closed. I heard mad heavy footsteps. " Lano" I asked scared. He pushed open my bedroom door looking mad asf. "You fucking Quanny bitch" he asked. I was so caught off guard that he found out that quickly. "Who told you that" I said scared. "How many times hoe" he asked as he took off his shirt. I stared not knowing if he was tricking me or not. Slap! "Bitch you done for" he gritted out, ripping my dress off. " Please Lano, I'm sorry bae" I cried as he slapped me again. I hoped none of our neighbors heard. I thought briefly remembering the windows were open. Later on that night, I walked to the bathroom hurting all over. He was entertaining Kian. Kenya had called but I hurt too much to answer. I had a busted lip, black eye and he had raped my pussy and ass and mouth for hours while beating me. I made a call. "Hello" the sexy voice said. I whispered in fear "Cuz i'm on my way tomorrow".

36.YOU ARE UNDER ARREST

Beau: I made it at 5:43am Sat. I was so tired but so happy and excited to see my cuz Pamela and start my new journey. I left with out a fucking trace while Lano was locked up for beating my ass and sodomizing me. I hated him, he was a fucking monster and fuck Zaya! She had been calling me and talking shit "Bitch watch ya back" she said from an unknown number and i just hung up.

The night of him raping and beating Beau .

 I heard banging on the door. OMG! I thought smoking a blunt and I pulled on my silk robe naked underneath. "We need to see the young lady that resides here" I heard a deep male voice say. I was super scared as I hid in my closet. "Yall ain't got no muthafuckin warrant" Kian said walking behind the cop as the other cop kept Lano down stairs in his eyesight. I could hear them coming towards me as he searched and searched and he pulled me from under the pile of clothes. "Its okay, you're safe now" the handsome blk man said and i started crying in relief and fear. Kian gave me the evil eye. He was on the phone with Kenya. "Cuff em " the blk cop told the white cop. "He didn't do this" I lied. "Really, his hands have bites and scratches on the young lady. Even if you don't show up in court, the state will pick it up" the white cop promised. I got dressed quickly and made sure Kian and Delano heard me say he didn't do it over and over. They took him to jail and I got as many items as possible in my car.

I took the cash he had stashed at my place. Around $15,000. I called Quanny over and he wanted to fuck Delano up but i told him to let that shit go. He had a U-haul and he got my bedroom suite and furniture and a few other big items and I was out! Detroit here I come. Quanny and a few of his niggas had drove the U -Haul. Halfway there he drove my car while I napped. The last of the ride I drove while he napped. He was a cool ass guy friend I thought.

 We pulled up to a decent suburb area. The house was huge and new looking. It had a 3 car garage. Pam was doing it big. "Bihh open the door" I said. My sexy ass cousin came out and them niggas jaw fell open. Lol i thought, she always got that reaction i grinned as Quanny just stared in lust. "Bitch I just got done shaking this big ass" she said, walking sexy towards me as then we hugged lovingly. "I was wondering why you dressed so early" i said as the niggas brought in my luggage. "Umm where a nearby hotel and food, they tired and all of us hungry as fuck" i said pointing at them fine ass niggas Quanny brought along to help me move. "Shiddd they can stay right here and i'm cooking black eyed peas, cornbread and fried chicken, i'm hungry too" she said as she walked to the kitchen. All her ass cheeks were showing in her black booty shorts. "Bitch i want some of them, you look cute as fuck" i said admiring her extra thick body and beautiful face.

She turned around and faced me and she had tears falling. She held my hands and said "You is your name Beautiful , never let these niggas mar up your face so anotha nigga don't want you. I'm glad you are here now and I was the one that called the police on Delano. I still had your address and after you called me and said you were on your way and he had beat you, I called anonymously and I hugged her tight" I love you cousin" i said sincerely. We wiped our tears and she said "Here you do what the fuck you like and i dare a nigga or bitch to fuck wit you my baby"

They know PP out here in the D baby" she said turning straight gangsta bitch despite her feminine face and body. I know she was about her bread and no games. "Aye i wanna fuck that Quanny nigga" she whispered as we passed blunts around waiting for the food to get done and it was only like 7:30 am. She called over a few stripper friends that was cool as fuck. "He got some good dick cuz, you will enjoy it," I said and we gave each other a hi five. I sat back and enjoyed myself as them niggas got entertained with some Detroit strippers. I saw Quan and Pam slip off and after i ate, i went to my new temporary room that i couldn't really enjoy because of how sleepy i was....

The Next Day…

 "Bihhh get dressed, I want you to come to the store with me" Pam said through the door. "Okayyy give me 20 min cuz" I said. I loved my huge room with my own bathroom. Today i had to put my bedroom suite and furniture in storage. My temp room had a queen size pillowtop mattress. There was a cherry wood bed frame and dresser and vanity mirror with matching chair. I loved the beautiful hardwood floors that just shone and I had a huge flat screen mounted on the wall.

My bathroom was done up in Emerald green and black with matching towels and washcloths fully stocked with tissue, soap, body wash, toothpaste and new toothbrushes. I felt like royalty ..lolzzz.. I came down and it was all the niggas wit Quanny and the hoes. I said hi to everyone and gave my friend Quanny a hug. "We will be back bae" Pam said tonguing Quanny. We walked out and she said "Girl he fucked me a few times , i'ma feed everybody before they leave tomorrow" she said unlocking her Cherry red Escalade that was really nice. "Cuz, thank you for everything and i love you" i said sincerely. She grinned pretty "That's what family is for cousin".

37. New Life In Detroit, Mi

Beautiful: Quanny made it back safe" i told Pam. "Im glad my boo made it back straight " she grinned. We had some niggas coming through later. My black eye still looked a mess but i had some bomb ass concealer so i was good and my lip was almost normal again. Delano had been blowing up my phone so i put him on the reject call list. When the investigation people called i made it clear i was good and i wasn't pressing charges and i was out of the state.

Delano had me scared as fuck of him. I wanted no problems with him. I was already feeling free to do as i pleased. Kenya had tried to contact me through email and i would respond later when i settled in. I wanted her to come and at least visit. Pam said she had no problem with Kenya coming and she was always looking for hoes to recruit.

Kenya was a bitch about that money but Kian fuck boi ass was so abusive and mean to my friend.

Lianna: "Bitch that nigga thinks this his fuckin baby but i have no idea who's it is Lita" i laughed smoking the blunt. "Girl be careful because Them niggas will kill you for shit like that bitch" Lita said. I liked getting my ass beating time to time. I had been really doing some foul shit lately. I had let Delano talk me into Escorting. I made so much money but i was putting so many miles on my pregnant pussy. I loved fucking married couples the most but i knew the way i earned money was not moral. I loved fucking the men with the pregnancy fetish. They actually made love to me as they fantasized I was pregnant for them. Sick right?

But I loved it. I met a new client that loves kissing and sucking lactating breasts as he fingered my asshole. I like him. I loved fucking mostly rich guys for a living and my boyfriend setting up the dates safely and handling the money. I just hated that Beau bitch, she had his heart. He jumped to her every spoiled dumb command. Los, my brother had been so upset when he found out we was still fucking. Oh well. "Bitch you still there " Lita said "Lita let me call this nigga and see where he at" i said sipping my beer. I only would have two since I was pregnant. I prayed that this baby was Delano's just to hurt that blk hoe Beautiful.

Delano :That hoe was gone! I went by her parents store several times and she wasn't there. I would stalk her parents house and i would call from different numbers and she never answered. I texted her over and over. I was gonna find her . She thought she was gonna fuck whoever she wanted and do whatever she wanted. Hell naw, she was my muthafuckin property.

When i find that bitch, ima torture her i thought in rage as i raped the 16 year old bitch. Her mom had sold her for dope and i always got first dibs. She was a virgin and a pretty mixed bitch. Her white mom sold her for a few heroin packs. "Shut the fuck up" i said thrusting in and out her small pussy. "Pleasssse it hurt sooo baddddd" she cried. Because I was mad Beautiful got away, I choked her as I raped her.

She would be a whore like the rest of these bitches i thought cumming in her pussy. "Now you know how to take a big black dick" I said sliding out of her. I kinda felt bad and threw three hundred dollars on her balled up frame as she cried softly. Oh well, this life i thought walking out the crack house.

Beautiful : Ooh he fine as hell i thought as i stood next to Pam. She had a party in my honor and it was a gang of muthafuckas here. I had my eyes on a sexy ass nucca. Bihhh you know i was stuntin on dem hoes. I was done with them chocolate niggas for a minute i thought as i lusted over this fine ass light skin nucca. He walked up and I looked away and struck up a convo with the nearest person. "Hey you a sexy ass bitch, i wanna fuck you" the stranger said and i giggled.

"What's your name yo" he said and his eyes was sexy as fuck deepset and dark with thick eyebrows and he was in the beard game. Sexy sexy sexy. I licked my lips "Beautiful and yours" I asked. "Jaceon, how long are you here for, I wanna take you out" he said charmingly with a set of white teeth behind those big pink pussy eating lips. "I'ma be here long enough" I flirted. He grinned "Well let me take you to breakfast then" he said. "I might" I said.

We clicked and i knew he would probably be the first nigga i fuck in the D. These niggas was so thirsty and not used to a bad bitch as myself. Pam was bad but BEAUTIFUL IS A BAD BITCH i thought checking myself in the body length mirror after i peed. Yeah i think i was gonna like Detroit i grinned as i walked back down to the party. Fuck Delano!

38. Being Found Out!

Beau: I was paranoid as fuck when I was out on public. Delano was stalking me on social media and Kenya was relaying info to me. Lianna had come over his place and tried to be cool with her. "Bihh, she was asking where you were and she had no hard feelings against you" Kenya told me and I laughed. "Delano is sick you left him and he is asking me have i heard from you" she said. "Don't tell them shit!" I said. "How you holding up girl?" I asked her. "Girl, Kian was his usual controlling crazy self" she said.

I told her about my new friend Jaceon. Jaceon wanted me to be his woman but I wanted to be single. We did fuck and it was good but he wanted more. "Be my woman" he had said after we fucked. "Can you let me up though" I asked as he was still between my thighs still and his condom covered dick inside me.

 It had only been a few weeks we had been fucking and he was already whipped on this southern style pussy. We e-mailed instead of texting so Kian wouldn't read. Kenya also told me that Delano was snorting powder with Lianna and running a small escort service. Damn, this nigga wilding out i thought. I had seen him toot Coke but had never I never did it. I made plans to go to a concert with Jaceon on Saturday and I was excited. I had been doing me. I had no idea if i wanted a decent job or just to fuck my way to the top and occasionally dance for extra cash. I had did a party with Pam and a couple other strippers in tiny bikinis and we danced and flirted with all the 22 men there. We left after 3 hours and I was $1100 richer. It was so fun being young, beautiful and a real authentic sexy curvy body. I called my parents and told them lies. "Yes school is going great" i lied. I felt bad but this was my life.

2 months later

"Girl tell that nigga we making money" Pam said to me. We were at another after party dancing in barely nothing and money was being thrown all over us but I tried to answer the call i was getting as I discreetly walked to an empty room slightly sweating. "Hello" I answered. "I found you BITCH" the voice said and hung up. Damn! I hope this nigga hadn't found me. I tried Kenya phone and I hadn't heard from her in weeks.

Kian had been beating her ass consistently and now she was pregnant again. I had no idea how my friend was doing. Did she tell Delano where I was at?? That had to be him. Well, he wouldn't be able to find me in big ass Detroit i thought as i twerked while on my knees as Pam stood over me and did the same dance move and the crowd of men cheered us on. I fell asleep at around 4am and i had the scariest dream of Delano finding me, raping me and killing me! I woke up in a sweat from fear. I needed to get my life together.

Delano: I went over to my brother's crib. Kian had caught Kenya e-mailing niggas and best of all Beautiful. The email said she was in Detroit Mi living with her cousin Pam. The bitch was dancing and fucking some nigga. I was gonna visit the D real soon and get my bitch back, I thought snorting a couple lines of Cocaine. It made me think clearer. Lianna had turned me on to it and I loved how it made me feel. It kept my dick hard also. Lianna had recruited some new young dope head pretty hoes to fuck for money.

 I had gone completely underground and was making so much illegal money. I had one thing missing, my bitch. I hated the thought of her being happy and free from my authority. She needed a man like me to control her, beat her and love her. I dreamed of finding her and killing her for leaving me. The more Coke I did and the more emails I read between her and Kenya, the more I fantasized of finding Beau and choking her to death while loving the fear I saw in her eyes as she slowly died. She had told Kenya over and over how scared she was of me and she was now fucking different men and could do as she pleased.

Fucking black hoe! I was gonna find her and fuck her up. Not kill her but really fuck her up i thought as my brother opened the door. "Damn" I yelled seeing Kenya beat up badly. She was limping as she fried chicken and had pots on the stove. I smelled greens and black eyed peas and cornbread. He waved me down to the living room which was humongous. We sat and smoked a blunt.

 "I'm going to make a move in Detroit next weekend bro" he said grinning evilly. He hated disobedient bitches. He wanted me to teach Beau a lesson. "Bro i can finally get that hoe for everything she did to me" i said and he nodded pulling out a vial of Coke, I got it for you after giving Hector an extra $20" he said and i laughed. Oh yeah Beau, im gonna fuck you up i thought as my dick hardened. Kian and I got high as shit off weed and coke and Henny as we made plans to visit Detroit.

39. Back To Reality...

Beau: "Jaceon, i do want to meet your family eventually, i'm just not ready yet" i said as we laid in his bed. He was such a sweetheart. He was in love with me and I was in love with MONEY. Pam and I had started a small business dancing for after parties and whatever and whoever else. I was banking a lot of money and had plans to open a strip club with a few investors. Kenya emailed me from a crazy email name and told me Delano was in Detroit and to watch out. That had been a couple of months ago. I still had nightmares of Delano finding me.

I never went out alone and I was just plain paranoid of everyone and everything. I was thinking of moving to another part of Michigan since she said he had read our emails and knew I was in Detroit. I should've never fucked with him i thought as i showered for a new day.

I meditated for 20 minutes to help my anxiety. I got dressed to actually apply for college classes. I was headed down a destructive lifestyle if i wasn't careful so i decided to enroll in classes until i moved away. All I did was party party party. Pam was all about fucking niggas and money. She was really a cold hearted whore I saw as she encouraged me to escort. I was planning to move out of her place. I loved her but she was negative. I felt bad for lying to my parents also. I walked out the door after saying bye to a sleepy Pam knocked out naked on her big firm couch drunk as fuck. It was still kinda dark at 4:45 am and I had a 2 hour drive. The hairs on the back of my neck stood up as I felt a presence and then I saw darkness fast.

3 days later

 I woke up being raped. He was keeping me drugged up. He was on top of me "Bitch i found you" he gritted out fucking me hard. I moaned as my head hurt from being hit in the head. I was naked in a bed as this crazy ass nigga told me "I own you bitch!" as he ejaculated inside me. I almost threw up with fear. He got up and sat at the small table in the nice motel room.

He had a bag of Coke and he was now snorting some. I was shaking with fear. "Lano, I'm sorry but I left so the police wouldn't keep me going to court against you" I said which was partly true. He was still looking super fine and sexy but his eyes were different from the drugs. "Shut the fuck up slut, i know you fucking hate me!" he yelled mad.

He was a Coke monster! I was glad I had my Apple watch on. I could make a call when he left the room I thought as he degraded me and went through my cell after I gave him my pin to unlock it. "You fucking nasty slut!" he yelled slapping me and i cried out tasting blood, pissing on myself it hurt so bad. "Get the fuck up bitch and go bathe" he said disgusted. I hurt so bad but I moved with lightning speed.

I used the app on my watch and dialed the police. I was running the shower as he got new linen for the bed I soiled. I was in the shower with my back to the water as I talked low in a whisper. "What the Fuck you doing" he said snatching back the shower door. "I was praying you would forgive me" I said , making him laugh and walk out the bathroom with my phone in his back pants pocket.

 I got out minutes later hoping the police had heard him. I felt my eye closed and swollen and it looked terrible in the mirror. I wore a sheet around me as he ordered breakfast. "You're coming back home and you're gonna be my secret slave" he grinned evilly. "Can I say bye to my Pam" I asked. "Fuck that bitch, she bad influence on you" he said snorting a few lines. When did he get to be such a big Coke head I wondered. He probably had been doing that shit longer than what I knew. He always had a temper and seemed moody. I finally heard a loud Knock Knock Knock! "Police, open the door!" we both heard. "I knew that muthafucka was acting weird" he said of the dude who brought us breakfast. I was scared and relieved. He opened the door saying it was just him as I hid as he told me. I heard them slam him to the floor and call out my name "Beautiful come out, we got a call you are in here" a deep voice with authority said. They found me in the tub crying and beat up. The officer walked me out and the other officers shook their heads in pity at the way I looked. I finally fell asleep after days of being raped and abused by Delano.

2 Days later

 I got my cell back and I called my mom. "Oh Lis! We were so scared baby, are you okay" my mom asked over the phone with fear in her voice. "Mom i love you and dad and I wanna come home and do the right things and be a good person" i cried. I was in the Critical Care unit. I had to have reconstructive face surgery and I had lost several teeth. I was happy to be alive. I also was scared straight.

 I just wanted to be a young educated lady and live righteous. Yes I would hang out here and there but i was done with wanting the fast money. I had learned my lesson. I went and packed all my things a week later with bandages everywhere and I thanked Pam for letting me come stay with her but I was heading home. I left Detroit behind and that lifestyle I was living.

4 yrs later...

I walked across that stage acting up. I was graduating from college and I was so excited for my new life. Yes Bitch! I did that. I was moving to California for my internship at a reputable company. They would hire me after 3 months of internship to making $85,000 a year. I had moved back in with my parents, signed up for college and was accepted at a university nearby.

 I did all four years on the honor roll. I had some difficulties with having several procedures on my face. I had permanently lost eyesight in my left eye which I wore designer frames to hide. Delano had gotten 43 years for what he did to me and his prostitute ring. I also heard Kenya was still with Kian and they had moved out of town. I was now a woman with experiences and more to come i thought excitedly.

Outro:

 Beautiful moved on to become a successful millionaire and married a slightly older man who owned a law firm. He was a black man who was 40 and she was 27. They had a set of twin boys and a daughter. Beautiful felt that she actually had been lucky to start over and she cherished life and her loved ones.. She still was BEAUTIFUL AND OUT COLD!

The End! I dedicate all my books to my Beautiful readers. I Love You All So Very Much. Be Blessed.